Thinking Aloud About People & Beetles & Photographs

K. Michael Weaver

Published by Honeybee Books
www.honeybeebooks.co.uk

Printed in the UK using paper from sustainable sources

ISBN: 978-1-913675-28-8

The front cover image is courtesy of Max K. Weaver.

www.maxkweaver.com

For Max K Weaver again, who has my biggest love

Also, for Nick Skelton - aka DJ Skunk - my dear friend and great music buddy of thirty years. The go-to DJ for dancing

FOR MY READERS:

These pieces are about the all-sorts of this world.

A world that I love to unpick, unpack and wonder about, and then repack, through my writing.

All-sorts about:

The tiny fractions of other peoples' lives that I have witnessed and been fascinated by, compelling me to find a home for them in my fictions.

About life situations that I have faced myself, that I want to try and make sense of by writing them out of me, and then getting them out into the world onto a page and into a book.

About faces, eyes.

About noticing's.

About searching for things and finding things that aren't what they seem.

About looking and not being seen to be looking. About looking when you probably shouldn't look.

About how a moment in history is shared between a father and son.

About confession.

About mothers and daughters, when they want to remember the past.

About a lad who lived near me that worried too much and cried a great deal.

About another lad that rocked up unexpected & uninvited to a church one day, when I was planning my wedding with a woman that I loved.

About a strange situation played out on a strange island that doesn't exist, though the mothers and fathers and sons within it, do exist. They are known to me and three of them are my family.

The pieces for '***Thinking Aloud About People & Beetles & Photographs***' were written following a Bursary Award I received from The Cambridge Dark Room & Eastern Arts in 1994. A series of interviews were conducted with department heads at Cambridge University within the departments of medicine, archaeology, astronomy, nuclear physics, and forensics, who used photography to document aspects of their work.

I cannot remember now how I got from the notes and recordings made during these interviews to the actual writing of the piece itself. There is a connection of course, but I don't know what it is now, or was back then. I have truly forgotten this. I've allowed it to 'go home inside me', without logging and filing it properly in my memory. It is somewhere inside my head, but in a place that I can no longer find.

Is it a story I wonder, or something else entirely? If so, does this something else have a name, so that I could say to people 'I write these……'whatevers they ares' kinds of pieces, if anybody was to ask.

Maybe they are poems, but I don't think so, because I am not a poet.

The writing of '***A Fairy Tale For Torn Families***' was commissioned and written to be spoken aloud. It was indeed spoken aloud within an art installation by the Zwillinge Project in 1995 called 'Walled Garden' at the Bridgewater Arts Centre in Somerset. Do feel free to read it out loud yourself and to others if you want to.

I hope you enjoy my world. You are welcome to join me within it.

K. Michael Weaver

Contents

It’s About Who I Am, & He Is, & He Is

We find the remains of horses in the garden.

It is *our* garden.

There are the remains of horses and dogs. Of cows, of cats, and of birds. We find these splintered old spines and teeth, beaks, and skulls, in the middle of winter, when other fathers and sons are mostly huddled inside, marking time with the video remote control. I the father am thirty-five, and he the son is two-and-two quarters.

Now *I* like to explore, and so that is what, *we* like.

There are two of each of these things that have, at some point, eaten and slept, run, fucked and flown, but there are three horses, and so they are the exception. There is also everything else under the sun here to shame God, that God has nothing to do with, tangled and resting with their remains.

There are small things. Shapes of iron, copper, brass. Metal bits and pieces, indexed somewhere in a remaindered industrial manual. And what else? Again, small things. Babies’ clothes ripped and torn. Lumps of melted Mickey Mouse, lumps of Barbie and lumps of Pluto that have slimed their way onto the linings of a sagging assortment of adult male underpants. There are odd rotting working boots, leather uppers with plastic soles. And then there are big things. Mini-Cooper doors. Bikes. Engines. All knackered. What a picture. What a bloody awful picture.

So, there is a father and a son searching.

Sifting.

Searching for goodness to surface from *their* garden.

We stop, every so often. Stop for a drink and a biscuit. We sit together on a thick blue plastic sheet, laid out on the good earth. On this sheet, there is just enough room for both our bums. Our Wellington boots and our bits of bare leg resting out across the ground, amongst the ants, beetles, and worms.

We drink, suck our biscuits, and talk. What about? What do two males, who are separated in years by nearly thirty-two, say to one another? Two and two quarters as yet, has only a handful of words. He tries this handful out in all sorts of combinations, playing around with sense. I, the old one, talk about my own father, sharing secrets and woes with myself and my son.

I indulge in complaints, but Little Man talks about what is happening now, where he is at this moment, and what the hell is going on. He talks about his good biscuit and his good drink. He talks about the running that his nose is doing, and he asks about the steam that's pouring out of his mouth into the cold air, because it's great fun and frightening at the same time. I understand what he's saying, in spite of his half-a-dozen dictionary. It makes my heart turn, because it's about where we are, and what we're doing. There is no patina of regret in his words, such as they are.

Innocent eyes in the world are things to be cherished.

I, the old one, talk about my father. It seems like now is the right time to do the comparing of certain fathers with certain sons, and to share this comparison with Little Man, my son.

This is a real adventure were having, even though there are strange male underpants staring both of us in the face. We suck our biscuits and talk, in our ways, our very different ways, and smear muddy hands across cold white faces. Laughing together.

November in the garden.

I remember my father.

Don't get me wrong - he isn't dead.

No.

But I *remember* him.

Michael is his name. Michael doesn't like the sun. He doesn't like arriving anywhere early or late. Michael is seventy-five. He used to boil ants to death with water, when they appeared in concrete cracks - I remember this from when I was his Little Man.

I want to tell you that I have never heard Michael scream. I wonder what that must sound like? My father screaming into the night. What, I wonder, would be the position of his face for screaming? I just can't picture it at all.

My Michael has no friends, but many acquaintances, who I'm certain think him idiotic. My Michael is neurotically in fear of debt. But that's enough of him. In fact, that's a bit too much enough of him.

Okay. Little Man, my Little Man.

No. That's unkind.

Max.

Max and I have our spades.

We're sorting through the things that matter, and the things that don't. He chooses things that I wouldn't, and vice versa. He has a pile, and I have a pile. I can't work out his collecting logic, and he seems disinterested in mine.

He has a dolls head, with the lipstick still intact. He has a piece of green sponge that isn't a shape that has a name, though he thinks it's a triangle, and he has a plastic bucket, without a bottom to it which, at not regular intervals, he fills with earth and then hauls, of course empty, to the blue plastic sheet where we park our bums whenever the fancy takes me.

He works so incredibly hard. Harder than I do. Breaking out in a workman's sweat at two-and-two-quarters. He attempts many things that are impossible because he doesn't know that they're impossible. I like that. He has a world going on that I used to live in, but where the hell did that fly off to, I wonder? And when?

I am collecting and arranging in their blue-print shape, the teeth and spines and ribs and jaws of certain things that I know. I know the shape that these things used to be when they were grazing, and flying, and chasing each other for fun, or something more serious. Without their skin and organs on, I can still understand what they are.

I put them back together, for Max, joint by joint, laying them out like stencils in an already cleared part of the garden. Lay them out in their shape, for my son to marvel at.

I say to Max, 'This is a horse.'

I say to him, 'This is a dog.'

I say to my son, 'This is a bird.'

And he laughs. He thinks that I'm having him on. If he could say, 'Don't be ridiculous Dad.', it would be at these moments that he would use these words. He knows a horse and a dog and a bird, and these old dead stencils on the ground aren't anything like any of them. I'm thinking whilst he's laughing at me - I'm thinking that I want to tell him that this is what he is like inside. As he stands there, sucking on his thumb, looking at a dead and gone horse. But how do you tell a child the truth when it's a truth about mortality?

He should be told though, shouldn't he?

A child's body, and being, is such a beautiful thing.

'Michael. Dad. Hey, you!'

You're not here right now, but I want you to know that I'm saying this anyway. I want to tell you Dad that I do not love you. I want to tell you this because I haven't a fucking clue who you are. You know Max, my son. Your grandson. He adores Opi because of your curly sideburns. Because you are funny and fun to be with - hah bloody hah! What will my son Max, your grandson, get in his turn, because of the curdling mess that you and I are together? Eh Dad? I have lots of questions, but I'm not convinced that you have answers to many of them. Or any of them!

What do I want to know from you when I really think about it? Well, I'm in my garden with my son, and we're looking at something that is dead, just bones. We're having an adventure that involves discovering things that are dead. What do you think I should say to your grandson? Come on! Shake a leg mate. Why were the ants in concrete cracks such a problem for you? Eh Dad? The hours that you wasted. Pratting around. They just kept coming back. Year after year. Didn't they? And you never got the message. The message that I liked to watch them. Watch them living and doing what they do. Surfing on boiling water pissed them off. Pissed me off. Adventures with ants - that's what I wanted. Stories from you about fantastic ants.

But you Max. To return to you. Max. That's the name that we gave you. Max, and the rest, that middle name Lawrence. What are we like us parents?

You should know that Max is the name of a woman that I once loved, and that Lawrence is the name of your mother's dead brother. Lawrence died young, and it was a sorry situation. A situation of suicide. I want to remember her, that lover, and your mother wants to remember him, that brother, which is why you are who you are. Your mother felt threatened by her, and I never knew him. Your name is situated in this strange vein of loyalty and remembrance. I am in a garden with you, my son, and you are having an adventure - I can see that you are by the look on your face.

We stop what we're doing. Our sifting and searching. Because I've taken a slice out of my thumb. It was my sucking thumb when I was two and two quarters like you. It's a sharp lump of Marmite jar, sitting in my thumb, trying to feed me its goodness. Years-old yeast extract, forging its way into my hand. You're watching very closely. Your daddy wincing, and then your daddy pinching glass out of his thumb skin. Then I suck the thumb, pulling blood across my tongue. You suck when you see me suck. We suck away together. You stroke your nose as well with a soft bent index finger for added affect.

I want to build a fire now and burn the year in and year out of all this stranger's trash that we have brought out into the light to make our garden good.

There is a week like this of unearthing dead animals. Beautiful things. Max helping in his way, with quarter-size plastic tools. There are buckets and barrows full of glass, an old greyhound shed, bags of clothes and just plain crap of the world exhumed along the way. Then it's skipped out of town, to add contour to hills that need a bit of grass sowing on them as a matter of urgency. Then there's a daily fire for all the mess that back garden bonfires can manage.

And then there's just a huge square of bare earth, with dead animals in the shape that they need to be, lying there, waiting for something to happen. Myself and my son standing on the bare earth, looking at stencils of other people's pets, large and small.

We're both wondering now.

Wondering what to do.

That night, when Max is dreaming, barking gently like a little dog, and laughing in his sleep, my father phones and we awkwardly do the talking together about nothing in particular, as we usually awkwardly do.

I joke. I tell him that I've buried Max out in the garden for the weekend. 'Will do him good to struggle for air', I say, so he'll realise that nothing is served to you on a plate in this world. I say this because I'm convinced that my father doesn't listen to anything that I say. He's always got half an eye on the small change jangling in his pocket. Half an eye on stray dogs soiling his lawns. Half an eye on making sure that all doors are locked securely. Half an eye on business brought into the house on the bottom of the Prudential Man's shoe. There are too many halves here to clock that son has left grandson struggling for air out in the night with the ants, worms, and beetles.

Max, do forgive me for this horrid little story, but it's a game I like to play with Opi.

And what do I remember, when my father and I stagger and splutter together down the phone line? Well, I remember days that were very wide. They weren't long days. They were wide.

When I was a child, this was how the days were.

Yes, there were these days yes, but there were also the thin tragic days that folded in on themselves. Days that had had all their air sucked from them. These days Max, were when my father played at being my father and my mother at one and the same time.

My mother was dragging herself into awkward corners, losing all of her lovely hair, as she had a breakdown very nervously. There was suddenly no hair anywhere. Mother had gone to the dogs in the hair department and what was I to think? Then there were standard wigs trussed by head scarves in the East coast wind on washing days. And mother sliding from room to room attempting magical acts of disappearance behind doors, in a house where her children might notice and wonder.

A mother vanished.

The wife of my father vanished.

What a hell of a thing to happen to my mother, the woman.

I've seen the photographs. She used to be Miss Faversham. A trailered float and pennies in the air for her beauty.

If I ever find God anywhere, I'll stamp on him/her, or it, for its cruelty to my mother.

But what's to be done with the bones of dead pets, large and small? They lay out there on the earth with no glory, and we venture to look at them, Max and I, each day over the weeks that follow. One day he says:

'The dinosaurs Dad.'

And he points up into the sky to where the moon was, the last time he saw it in the dark.

He's decided that this is where they come from, and that this is therefore where they need to return to.

I wonder if he thinks that this is where he comes from as well?

He jumbles across the earth, bends down, and gathers one of the horse skulls in his arms. This old head is almost as long as he is. His tiny hands grabbing at the horses top set of teeth, folding the head closely into his junior donkey jacket chest. He jumbles back to where I'm standing and then, with every bit of his might, he pushes Mrs. Horse up above his head and wobbles on the spot repeating over and over again:

'Up the sky Dad, up the sky.'

I can hear something rattling as he shakes the skull around, trying to push it up and out to heaven. Then he stumbles and falls, horse's skull first, cracking his own head against its cheek. Flailing about on the ground, trying to free his body from this old dead thing, he's suddenly frightened by it for the first time. His body doesn't want to be near it any longer but, trussed in his layers of clothes, it's difficult to get away. I pull it out from where he's struggling, and then help him to his feet. The skull rattles again when I pull it towards me from out amongst my son. There's a thumb of Max's, going into Max's mouth as he backs away fearful, and parks himself on the safety of the blue plastic sheet for break-times.

I'm shaking the skull now and it's still rattling. I turn it over and over in my hands, still shaking it, and then the rattling stops when I see something fall from it to the ground. There's a rusted bullet head sitting there on the earth of my garden. *Our* garden. This animal was shot dead in *our* garden.

'What do I do now Dad? This changes the whole complexion of things Dad, doesn't it? What kind of a garden is this for your grandson to play in, when a shooting has occurred?'

Now the horse must have been shot through the mouth or the eye or another natural hole, because there are no unnatural holes when I begin to search the skull for the bullets point of entry.

It's magical to unearth the remains of dead animals in a garden where your son will one day play on swings and grass, and probably amongst the vegetables, but does the same apply when a shooting has occurred?

I want to know the full story. I want to know the full extent of this other adventure that happened in *our* garden. I know that the horse was shot in the head, but I don't know all the story of the shooting. It's probably a simple one of age, and of a life being put out of its misery.

I would like to see the faces that were there though. The who, the how many, their faces, and the hand whose finger pulled the trigger before the animal dropped, or was it kneeling already?

How does a horse kneel gracefully? I don't suppose it does.

I don't suppose that God ever intended that a horse should kneel.

It's like the thing about men wanting to fly, but them not being able to without the jet engines.

The image of an old horse attempting to kneel as a man next to it attempts to leave the ground and fly. The one looking at the other anxiously. Each attempting to do the thing that they're attempting, subject to a gun at their head.

But it's easier for a horse to kneel than it is for a man to fly, or so it seems to me.

I need to do some proper thinking now, and to stop rambling.

This is a garden that I want you to play in Max. It can still be magical.

I'll get rid of the horse, and I'll stop imagining things that might have happened. These things in my head will make me want to watch out for you when you play. There wouldn't be any freedom for you. Not like that. Guns at the head of a horse and at the head of an imaginary man attempting to fly. You're two and two quarters and your little body, your little self, is a beautiful thing.

You have all my love Max.

But what is love?

My mother ran into my father when she was riding her bike.

This was how they met.

Had an accident in the road on a Thursday in Faversham and couldn't be pulled apart, so they got married.

Out in the world near Faversham, two sisters are hiding and struggling for air. Five strangers who had to live together for part of their lives.

My father taps a lot when I'm with him. Taps his knees with his fingers. Taps his lips with other fingers. I don't understand the code. I don't understand what his messages are, and there is nothing in the words that he uses with me to prove that he is a father. I think that one day he'll turn into a butterfly and fly off into the sun, even though he hates the sun. I'll hopefully be there to watch and wave and wonder what we were all about. It was a tangled mess for years and years and then he simply just flew off into the sun. A sun that he hated.

In the garden, the horse has gone.

I've taken it away.

All the horses have gone, and Max and I agree that we're having an adventure again.

He wants a pond, like the one he's seen at Omi and Opi's.

Inside his head, I can see these words forming:

'There's lots of digging to be done Dad, so don't just stand there, looking like my Dad. I like the dogs and cows and cats and birds. They can all stay, but get on with the pond will you.

The earth's coming out of the earth and Dad is digging his disappearing into my pond, with fish and frogs to come, I hope. I want to come down so that I'm in my pond. So that I can't see out unless it's only what is straight up to the sky. Because it's *my* pond, I want what I want. Please.'

'Max. Move out of the way. There is something there under your boot. Under your boot. This is not a game. Move out of the way. Up you go. Stand by that tree over there, there's a good boy.

Good boy.

Good boy.

Good boy.'

I'm standing quietly.

Just looking.

I'm looking down to where Max's boot has just been.

Looking from there to Max's face.

A face trembling by the tree.

The air is being sucked out of this day because:

I find the remains of a strange child's hand in our garden.

Where *our* pond wanted to be.

The bones of a hand.

Of hands, and the bones from every part of this child.

This child's body was a beautiful thing.
It was a beautiful thing, but its bones could never be magical.
Not like the bones of horses.
Of dogs.
Of cows.
Of cats.
And of birds.

What can I tell you about the future Max?

Well, I can tell you that when you are sixteen, I will be forty-seven.
When you are eighteen, I will be forty-nine.
And when you are twenty-one, I will be fifty-two.

It will be an adventure, but we'll really have to try hard, wont we?

Thinking Aloud About People, & Beetles, & Photographs

These are just a few thoughts that are keeping me company.

They're keeping me company.

At the moment.

A first thought is a thought about faces:

Faces don't exist anywhere else but here.

There are no faces through a microscope, and there are never faces through a telescope. Faces don't exist, anywhere else but here.

Perhaps this is why faces are so valuable?

His face is hidden beneath a black hood, since he is about to be shot.

Her face is hidden beneath a black veil because her child has recently died.

His face is hidden beneath a pale stockinged mask - he wants things that do not belong to him.

His face is hidden beneath a nice check travelling blanket and he travels with lots of other men in a car that is driven very fast - he is probably the source for a public outrage.

His face is hidden beneath his Bat mask - he is very rich and therefore able to do lots of good things without being paid for them. He is also seen in a car that is driven very fast but, it is him that drives it, and there are not lots of other men in the car to keep him company.

Faces don't exist anywhere else but here, and it is sometimes necessary to hide them because they are so valuable.

This is another thought, and it is about eyes:

This is an introduction, a short introduction, to my friend's eye.

It is a large eye. Yes. A large blue eye. My friend calls it his 'Eye for Detail'. His other eye is also blue, and it is large as well, but he doesn't call it anything in particular. So, I call it his 'Eye for Doing Whatever He Wants With'.

Anyway, his 'Eye for Detail' is the same shade of blue as a little ball that I had as a child. I used to use the ball to do lots of very interesting things with, and I used to call these very interesting things my 'Experiments for Finding Out'. I spent lots of time throwing the ball, just throwing it. Throwing it sometimes on purpose, knowing where it would land, and other times I'd throw it without thinking, just to see where it would come to rest without me wanting it to stop here or there. The blue ball was my passport to lots of hidden and mostly very awkward but interesting places. Places like the underneath of cars parked in the street. Places like our shed roof and the rock garden in the middle of next door's pond. And places like the cellar in our house that smelt like my grandfather.

My grandfather had only one eye because, as he told me once, he lost the other one in the war. Since my grandfather was always a very clumsy and accident-prone man, I think that he was lucky only to have lost one of his eyes.

I remember that he had a friend too, and that one day, I overheard the friend saying to him:

'I lost my wife yesterday'.

Neither of them said anything to one another for a long while after those words were spoken. They just stood looking at one another very closely. Their look was a 'Finding Out' look, but I don't think that they discovered anything new, like what was underneath cars parked in the street, like what the shed roof had to offer. Their look was not an experiment like mine, and it didn't seem nearly as much fun.

The next time that I saw my grandfather's friend after that was on the front page of the local newspaper the following week. He looked quite a lot younger in the photograph, but it was definitely him. It showed my grandfather's friend - he was dressed in a blue suit. The caption in bold type beneath the picture read, MAN COMMITS SUICIDE OF A BROKEN HEART.

I keep expecting to see a photograph of my grandfather in the same weekly paper because he is very old now and doesn't seem to want to find things out anymore. He even says sometimes:

'I've found out all I need to know thank you very much'.

My grandfather is sometimes able to say this, without actually saying anything.

I can see it in his eyes though.

This is a thought, about being six:

I am six, and I have a beetle, a beetle that lives on my hand. I make shapes with my hand for beetle. A great many shapes, for beetle's great many travellings. He crosses the world of my hand, and each time he does this, the world is slightly different for him. This happens for many days, and then the day of the big expedition comes.

I ask beetle if he would like to go to the moon.

He doesn't say yes, and he doesn't say no, so we go anyway.

On the bus.

On the bus, to one of those huge buildings that go to the sky.

Buildings with lots of glass, for giants to catch their reflections in.

Now, I don't know any giants, so me and beetle must take the lift.

There are two lifts, one beside the other. Their doors open together, and they are both empty. I knock beetle off my hand into one of the lifts and press the button with the biggest number on it. The door closes and I hear beetle on his way. I take the other lift and press the button with the same big number on it.

There is some time when there is just a humming sound, like our fridge.

Then my door opens, and I step out onto the floor that is the big number on the buttons. Beetle seems to know about lifts because he is waiting on the floor in front of the lift door next to mine. I make an easy shape with my hand for beetle, and we walk together to the sign with the word 'ROOF' in big red letters on it. There is a door there, which I can just about reach to open. Then there is night-time, and it is very, very, very still.

There is a big white circle in the sky.

Beetle is very still on the end of my finger.

I put my finger and beetle up to the moon.

There is a tiny beetle on my finger on the moon.

But perhaps only giants would understand this.

This is a thought, and it is about a game:

I know this game and it is a very good one.

It's called 'Tell Me What This Is?'

And you play it with a blindfold on.

Sometimes, winning the game is impossible, but it certainly makes you think hard about what is in the world.

What you do is this. You get someone to blindfold you first of all, in a room that you mustn't have been to before.

A room with lots of things in it.

Then you ask them to spin you round and round with your blindfold on, just to be on the safe side. Eventually you fall on the floor, and I suppose that this is part of the game really.

Anyway, what they need to do then is this. Well, there are two choices really. One choice is this. They can lead you across the room and place one of your hands very carefully on a part of something that is in the room. With objects that are very big and heavy, this choice is the best one to make. With the other choice, they leave you standing very dizzy in the room and bring the thing to you which they then place against one of your hands with very great care.

The question that they then ask you is this:

'Tell Me What This Is?'

I have played this game a great deal, and I think I have only been right once. This was when the person that I was playing it with put his hand in mine and said: 'Tell Me What This Is?'

I have made lots of mistakes, but one thing I have learnt, is not to take things for granted.

In various games of 'Tell Me What This Is?', these things have happened:

When the centre of my palm was placed against one of the corners of a fridge I said, 'This is the ball-point of a ball-point pen.' When my whole hand was pressed around the neck of a stuffed swan I said, 'This is the leg of one of my sisters' favourite toys.' When the end of my biggest finger was pressed against the end of my girlfriend's nose, I said, 'This is a very comfortable sofa.' When both my palms were placed flat against the surface of a photograph mounted behind glass, a photograph of a child in a coffin, I said 'This is the window of my back door and if I could see, I would probably see this: a strange man leaving by the garden gate, carrying my grandfather's savings with him.'

I played the game for a long time, until I grew out of it, or it grew out of me.

I'm not sure which is the truth now.

This thought is about shopping:

I went into a shop, and I said this: 'I would like to buy a bicycle.' The shop in which I said this was a bicycle shop and there were hundreds and hundreds of bikes in it. Bikes standing upright on the floor. Bikes attached to the walls, and bikes hanging from the ceiling of the shop.

I had thought that buying a bicycle from such a shop would be easy, but there was something about the face of the person that I was speaking to, which soon made me realise that easy it would not be.

What did I want a bike for? Well, for getting from places on it, to different places. My need was a very simple one. The person in the shop with the strange face had information for me about bicycles, information vast and wide-ranging.

Now I know what a bicycle looks like:

It has two wheels, a frame, a chain, pedals, handlebars, and a saddle.

That was what I wanted.

Something that had all of these things, so that I could get from places on it, to different places.

Somehow though, this was not good enough for the person with bicycle information vast and wide-ranging on the end of his tongue.

I began to think that perhaps he was employed to sell something far more complicated than the thing which I wanted to buy.

He talked in a language that perhaps only bikes understand.

But I wasn't a bike.

I think he kept forgetting this, so I had to remind him several times which seemed to make him angry.

I wasn't a bike myself, I simply wanted to buy one.

What is it about bikes, that makes them so difficult to buy?

The bike man talked a great deal and then when I reminded him for perhaps the sixth or seventh time that I was not a bike myself, he led me towards the door of the shop, showering me with armfuls of literature about bikes, suggesting that perhaps I needed more time to think.

Now, as I have plenty of time to think anyway, I wasn't exactly sure what he was getting at.

He opened the shop door and made a movement with one of his arms that I had seen in films where one person wishes another to leave. I was then outside of the shop, with him still inside behind the closed shop door.

All of the bikes of course were still inside with him, and I had my armfuls of literature to deal with.

I noticed that there were many people riding bikes along the street. These people must be very clever I thought, to have got their bikes from shops like the one that I had just been in, out onto the road.

I assumed that, like me, they must have once carried armfuls of literature home with them on the bus.

I remember thinking when I was actually on the bus myself, that the other people on it with me, should perhaps consider extending their season tickets, because finding other means of transport is clearly a very time consuming and complicated business.

This thought is about something that I don't think is very nice:

This is something that I want to remember because it is about laughing.

It is about laughing very loudly.

It is about laughing very loudly last of all, but first of all, it is about a big street in the city and me walking along it, minding my own business.

Sometimes it is not possible though to do this for very long, without my own business, becoming 'Somebody else's business.

On this day, the laughing very loudly day, somebody else, was called Annette - it said so at the bottom of the shiny beige card that she forced into my hand as she approached me with her:

American accent.

With her beauty.

And with her very expensive looking winter coat.

The shiny beige card made its way very neatly into the palm of my hand, and later into the darkness at the back of my wallet.

There is no laughing yet.

This is still to come.

Annette fixed a very big smile on her face. It was a persuading smile, and it worked - I started reading the other words that were written above her name on the shiny card. They read like this:

Do you ever think about?

1. The purpose of life.
2. The cause of human suffering.
3. Why history repeats itself.
4. Whether there is a spiritual world or not.
5. Where evil comes from.
6. How to create true relationships.
7. How we can know that God exists.
8. How to create a better world.

Then it read:

Come and discuss answers to these important questions.

I read my way down the card and arrived at Annette's name again. I looked up from the Annette on the card to the Annette with the very expensive looking winter coat standing in front of me. She was still smiling, but the mathematics of her smile had changed. They were not persuading me any longer but were now thanking me.

Then, while she was stuck in her thanking smile, this happened:

There was a screech of brakes, followed by a loud crash, just next to us in the road. Two motor cars suddenly in rather a mess. The man in the front car got out shouting. He dragged the man in the car behind him out into the road and still shouting very loudly, he started to punch the other driver in the face. Lots of blood appeared on his fists and then this happened:

There was a huge explosion from inside the big store that Annette and I were standing opposite. There was suddenly glass everywhere. In the road. Everywhere. Then there were people holding themselves in strange positions. Clutching their faces, clutching their legs and other parts of their bodies, wandering from the store out into the street.

I looked at Annette.

I looked at the man punching the other man.

I looked at the people holding themselves in strange positions.

I looked back for Annette, to see her very expensive looking winter coat running off up the street into the distance with her in it.

I looked down at my feet, and there were lots of the shiny beige cards like mine, scattered across the pavement. The set of questions on my card were multiplied on the cards at my feet.

'Come and discuss answers to these important questions.', they all said.

Annette and her expensive looking winter coat had now disappeared. She must have run off to speak to the people who had answers to these questions, I thought.

I began to laugh, as I pictured a big room in which men and women in expensive looking clothes write down these answers on expensive paper with expensive pens and pass the paper round in a circle that is never broken.

It just keeps going round and round.

I laughed very loudly when I thought about this.

The shiny beige card sits in the darkness at the back of my wallet.

Expensive looking clothes now tend to make me laugh. People that offer me things in the street now tend to make me laugh. When strangers give me persuading smiles or thanking smiles, I look around expecting to see men fighting, or people holding themselves in strange positions.

All of these things help me to remember a day on which I laughed, when nobody else was laughing.

This thought is about trees, and it is about people:

The best material for building a tree with, is wood. Material science, with all of its tests and all of its calculations, agrees that nature is right. Wood is best for a tree.

There are two people, and these two people are sitting together for the last time. Last times, like this one, are about little words such as, sad, and about phrases such as, 'I will always remember the pink room at that guest house in Glasgow when we made love a great deal and invented a story about some people that were far more interesting than we could ever be'.

Phrases like this, during last times, always seem necessary, but at the same time they fall very flat in the air, because they do not help the situation at all.

Last times, like this one, happen in a room that has become familiar to two people. A room in which some things have been packed away in boxes, and other things remain in their place for him to notice before he leaves.

He notices the big lot of sunlight that fills the room. He notices a tiny black beetle that is very still on the windowsill. He notices the angle that a large plant leans out into the room at, from its brass pot against the wall. He notices that the room smells of oranges, and he notices her face, that is saying things, without her actually saying anything.

He notices a little blue ball that rests against the skirting board beneath the window.

Yes, and the picture postcard of 'The Last Supper' by somebody very famous, on the stone mantel piece above the open fireplace. There are lots of doors in the picture for the people in it to leave by if they wish.

He looks at each of these things that he has noticed, and then he thinks about the many other and different places that himself and the woman have sat together:

Places like pavements, early in the morning, when they laughed.

Like in a boat on a lake when they both realised that they were each frightened of swans.

Like on a nice check travelling blanket, underneath a tree.

Sitting together in these places and others, until it is necessary that it be the last time.

What happens to the things that he notices in the room after he leaves it?

Well, the big lot of sunlight continues to fill the room for many days after he has gone - this will do things to the room and the things in it:

The beetle will move onto another place, or it may even die, which is more likely. The strange angle to the plant leaning out into the room will change. All of these things that he notices will not remain as they were, and for that matter, neither will he, after he has gone.

Just before he actually leaves, he says a number of other awkward and pointless things to the woman. Then, and without asking her, he raises a camera to his eye and takes a photograph that will capture the blue ball, the beetle, the strange angle to the plant, the picture postcard, and her face - a photograph that he will later place in the darkness at the back of his wallet.

Wood is best for a tree.

Trees are best made of wood.

And memories.

What are they best made of?

This is a very big thought, but it is also very short:

We are suddenly here, having not been here, and then we stop being here very suddenly, having been here.

I think that people who take photographs find this difficult to accept.

Various Tattoos

Tattoos: Beginning

Danny is a small boy who does nothing but cry.

He is not my child.

I see him do nothing but cry.

He crouches on a grass verge, holding his head or his arm or his leg. These might have been touched or snagged by a stick, or a ball, or a stone, or even the wind maybe, and he crouches and cries. He threatens his larger friends who laugh with fuck words and cunt words, and then he cries. He is crying out to blame anybody but himself for the pains that he feels.

He cries out for his mother and for his father, convinced that they might understand, but they are nowhere in evidence. He falls from his bike on purpose, to avoid nothing in particular, and heads for the tarmac, knees first. He tangles his 'T' shirt in the wire of a fence, again on purpose, and then runs away from it, to hear the rip in order that he can cry. He blames the fence out loud and then whacks it with a chrome towel rail that he carries with him everywhere to batter what needs to be battered.

I have never seen anybody cry as often as this boy does. He finds a beetle in a hedgerow just next to a grassy verge. For just a small moment, there is a joy at this micro living thing, until he invents that it has bitten him. He crushes it between his fingers, flicks the carcass at a friend and cries, shouting fuck and cunt just as if he'd lost a leg in a gang fight that he's invented inside his head.

This boy is pale and small. Bitten fingernails and bleached sore lips. Hair like a bag of nails. If there is nothing to cry about, he will pick a healed black scab from a knee, squeeze it so that it bleeds, and then trail a bloody leg from one end of the road to the other, the self-inflicted bloody leg just another occasion to squeeze out yet more tears. Every car that passes him in the road, fast or slow, reasonable, or reckless, is accused without trial of nearly knocking him down.

All people in cars are 'Bastards'.

All people on passing bikes are 'Wanker's', including me.

Everything is a reason to swear a name, or alternatively, a shoddy reason to cry.

This boy has a freckled face, and I would say he is probably nine or ten years old. There is something about these freckles that seem important - his round face that harbours' them, needs them for his crying face to look its best, to be as potent as it can be. Without these freckles he would be lost. They encourage adult sympathy. They do the job of attention that he's asking for.

I don't know why this small boy needs to cry so often. His despair is housed just a few front doors away from my own front door.

He throws empty sweet wrappers and potato crisp packets into my front garden, in the hope perhaps that I might shout at him, so that perhaps he can then in turn shout back at me, so that we can then shout at one another, until the cows come home and until the shouting forces his tears.

I have the feeling that he has grown to despise me, because I do not shout at him, because I will not shout at him.

I have the feeling that very soon, he will begin to shout at me, simply because I choose not to shout at him.

My lack of reaction to this small boy pisses him off - I can see this in his eyes.

I am convinced that he will come purposefully to find me in an alleyway one day, when he is much older and stronger and when I am much older and probably weaker.

He will remember my face, will remember that I was the man who watched him crying, when he was just a small boy, with a freckled face. He will probably despise my age and my weakness.

I can expect him to spit on me, more than likely.
And maybe, I'll even see that chrome towel rail again, or something similar, with which he will knock the living daylights from me.

Tattoos: Middle

OOOOOO
OOOOOOOOO
OOOOOOOOOO
OOOOOOOOOOOO
OOOOOOOOOOOOO

Resting on a shelf, in front of my bathroom window, there are fifty cardboard toilet roll cores. Within each one of them, there is a small forest of dust. Within each one of them, there is also a bee or a butterfly or a wasp or a lady bird or a beetle that is dead - these are dead things that I have come across whilst cleaning the house.

Looking closely at them, it is not obvious why they have died. There are no obvious injuries to be seen. There are the right number of legs or wings or other body parts on each one of them. Their lives have simply stopped at some point, perhaps behind a cupboard, in a drawer, on a windowsill, in an abandoned web, inside an infrequently worn shoe, in a pocket, or underneath a bed.

Tattoos: End

My father maintained De Havilland Mosquito aircraft during the Second World War. He maintained them then with such passion, and with such commitment, that he is now unable to talk about little else, some fifty years on. He talks about their beauty, both on the ground, and in the air. He talks about the beauty and agility of an aircraft that he himself never flew.

I remember, as a child, building an Air-Fix model of a De Havilland Mosquito or a 'Mozzi', as my father affectionately called them. I remember that he talked for ages about the cannon guns that this aircraft housed in its nose cone and how it was his job to maintain these as well. I remember making that breathy shooting sound that lots of other boys when I was a child could make as well, as I flew the 'Mozzi' in my hand around my bedroom, or in the garden. The cannon guns on the model were thin and delicate and frequently got knocked off during my playing. This must have happened many many times, since many many times, I remember my father sitting at the kitchen table of an evening, under a very bright light, with reading glasses propped on his nose, gluing these cannons carefully back into place.

When I left home at sixteen, I came across this model 'Mozzi', at the bottom of a box, when I was packing away my childhood in the loft. The plastic of the model itself had discoloured with age. The coloured transfers were pealing from the 'Mozzis' fuselage. The cannon guns were barely visible, beneath a small nose-cone mountain of glue. I took this sad model plane with me when I left home, and kept it in a box, a box that has been moved along with me to the different houses that I have lived in since. Years later, on my fathers' seventy fifth birthday, I gave him the same model 'Mozzi' as his birthday present.

I thought it would be a good thing to do.

My father has never talked to me about living, about what it has been like for him to live his life, about what marks distinguish his life from anybody else's.

I have never seen him cry, or really laugh, have never really heard him talk about himself.

For years, he has been waiting for something to happen, whilst simply maintaining his life.

His body is better maintained than my own, though he is nearly twice my age.

He has looked after himself.

Right up until the moment that my father actually opened his seventy-fifth birthday present from me, I was sure that I was doing the right thing, that I was doing something good.

He pulled the tatty model 'Mozzi' out of the box that I'd specially decorated for it and placed the model on the table in front of him.

There were other presents already opened on this table as well:

handkerchiefs

a framed photograph of one of my sisters' recent children

a bonsai tree

a pair of fancy leather slippers

a wristwatch

a tin of Humbugs

a novel by John Le Carre

He sat and looked at these gifts that duly marked his particular moment of age.

He looked at them all for a very long time, before doing or saying anything.

Then he picked up an empty carrier bag from the floor at his feet, and one by one he put his gifts into the bag. He put all of his gifts into the bag, except for the model 'Mozzi', which remained on the table.

He handed the bag to me saying:

'You have these things because I don't really need them.'

Then he picked up the model plane from the tabletop, got up from his seat, and walked out into his garden through the open French windows of the sitting room.

He raised an arm in the air and suddenly had the model plane flying in his hand.

The breathy shooting sound that I had made as a child, he now drew out from inside of him.

He walked around the garden flying this old plane in his hand, making breathy shooting sounds as he walked.

I know that he knew that he was doing this, but I also know that he was crying, and that he didn't know that he was doing this as well.

His tears were coming from inside of him, but from a part of the inside of him that he didn't know himself.

A Fairy Tale For Torn Families

There are mothers and fathers and sons. No daughters. No daughters to be found anywhere. Once upon a time there are two mothers, two fathers and four sons. It makes a lovely picture, a lovely slice of time.

These once upon a time two mothers are hiding. Hiding, watching, and recording. With their eyes and long lens cameras. With charts and maps, pins and pens and rulers. It's a comfortable hiding time, in a comfortable hiding place. There are Irish linen sheets for their tired eyes when the mapping isn't happening. And there's plenty of cheese and fruit and brandy and piled high boxes of candy. They're hiding well these two mothers. Hiding from the fathers and sons.

The mothers are sometimes naked. And beautiful they are too.

They have their seats and desks and all their paraphernalia set behind the curtain of a two-way mirror. And what an enormous mirror it is. What with it being ten foot high, by twelve foot wide. It's set into a wall of course. One of the four walls of the beautiful room in which they have lived, live, and will live until the time is right for them to leave. There isn't a telephone line in this part of the land, but to compensate themselves for this lack, they have filled the room with the many other things that they love. There are flowers of every shade of colour and fragrance imaginable and there are their pets as well. A mole that is bigger than one would normally tolerate, a tortoise, a lizard, and an angel fish, who all get along just fine, don't ask me why. The pets live not exactly in the room, but beneath it, in the cellar. This is a dank and nasty place but there are few complaints. Well, none that the mothers have heard of late, that's for sure. The pets are well fed and who can ask for more than this, when there are the thousands who starve.

The mothers have their secret in the cellar as well, but I'll tell you what it is, because it's really very sad. It's a table tennis table, complete with two bats, a low net and a large bag of ping-pong balls. When the mothers tire of watching the fathers and sons through the large and handsome two-way mirror, they retire to the cellar to practice their forehands and backhands. It keeps them in trim. And of course, as one would expect, they are fiercely competitive. The best of three will usually extend to the best of five and way beyond even this sometimes if they're in the mood.

So, they watch and map and calculate from the movements of the fathers and sons, waiting for the time when they can leave. They have their beautiful things, in their spacious and exquisitely beautiful room and there's even their light entertainment as well. What more could a woman want?

The fathers and sons. Well, what of them? Who do they consist of, where are they, and how do they spend their days and nights? There are three natural sons and a stepson. This stepson likes to throw things. Rings and keys and stones, but mostly stones. Then there are the young boy twins who rush everywhere, try everything, and speak in their private language sometimes to the exclusion of all and everything else. And lastly, there is the good one, the son who does all that he does in moderation. He has been good for all time, but there will come a time, his father believes, when he will assume the face and actions of a tyrant and lead himself into temptation.

The fathers like to do what is best for their sons, so the days that they are together are spent playing and eating and laughing, out in the good air under the sky. Nobody knows where the mothers have gone, so the fathers tell their sons, in carefully thought through chapters, story after story about fantastic disappearing mothers. Mothers who have double lives, who can transform themselves into jewelled express trains and journey out across the world to do the things that make them happy. To do the things that pay the bills.

You can see the fathers and sons. And they can see themselves. It is the beginning of another day like any other. The reflections of two men and four boys of different heights caught in the light of a mirror, a mirror ten foot high and twelve foot wide.

Each of their days begins like this, with an inspection of their own reflections. They treat it like a game, a game that's called, 'What Do You Notice That's Different?'. The boys and the men point out to one another the things that have changed from one day to the next. A bruise that wasn't there yesterday, but that is there today; on an arm, or a leg, or a face, or a spot, or a wrinkle that's new. This is always what happens first, and then the happy party play their second game called, 'Hunt The Way In'. You see, the mirror that they inspect themselves in, is set into one of the four walls of a huge square building that has no door or windows, no entrance.

In much the same way that the appearance of the men and boys' changes slightly each day, in turn, the men and boys believe that this huge sad building will change. That one day the beginnings of a door will appear in one of its walls. First perhaps just a crack, that in the days that follow might lead itself to form the shape of a door. Then a hinge and two hinges. Then finally a handle to turn, so that all inside can be revealed, in whatever glory it has.

This is what they believe, and this is why they, 'Hunt the Way In', with their eyes and fingers around the building, always laughing as they go.

This building stands in a field. A green field. Green field everywhere, on every side, for as far as the eye can see. For as far as the eyes of the mothers can see and for as far as the eyes of the fathers and sons can see. This is all that there is, except for a pile of stones, the height of a man, that stands in the field. That stands in the field at a stone's throw from the building in which the mothers are watching, keeping their eyes peeled for a time when it will be safe for them to leave.

Now fathers and sons will be men and boys when it comes to a pile of stones. And if all that there is to play with is a pile of stones, then you'd better use your imagination hadn't you, otherwise the days will get long and tedious wont they, don't you know? You see, the fathers are not aware of the limits of the green land on which they spend their days with all the happy sons. All that they have ever seen is green, apart from the stones and that building that they and their sons look at themselves in, day after day after day. That of course, and the blue of the sky, but then blue isn't so very different from green. Not when you come to think about it.

And so, on a particular day, when they imagine that they and their sons are at last ready to undertake the biggest of all adventures, they announce the game called, 'Let's Find the Limits To Our Land Boys, And Let's Use These Damn Stones In The Process Shall We?' It's not just about the stones though. This is not alone what prompts the biggest of all adventures. It's also about the gun shots in the sky above them that they have heard, on a daily basis, for as long as they can remember. At first, and this was long before the boys were born, when the fathers and mothers fucked together fancy free in the vast field of green, the fathers and mothers would huddle together for safety whenever a shot rang out in the sky above them. But the shots only and ever rained across this sky above and, little by little, they decided that the safe huddling together was unnecessary because nothing was being aimed at these good people down below where all was green and fancy free.

But of course, the fathers continued to wonder for years and years. Then there were boys coming out into the light from inside of the mothers and then, after a period of weaning, these mothers sadly disappearing into the darkness of night.

The fathers continued to wonder about the shots in the sky. In the biggest of all adventures, each father and each son carried a stone from the pile of stones. From when it was light to when it was dark, they would walk together in a straight line, outward from the pile of stones, walking together to find the limits of their green land.

On the first day it took them exactly a day to find where all things green ended.

Because suddenly there was the sea. But there wasn't only the sea. On the edge of the green land, where it met the sea, stood, what could only be described by the fathers, as an observation tower. A fortified hut on stilts, reaching up into the sky. Men could be seen by the fathers to be moving about in the tower.

The fathers called out to them, but the men in the tower were just too busy to notice the cries from below. At night, the fathers and sons would sleep on the green land by the sea, resting their heads on the stones that they had brought with them.

The following morning, leaving their hard pillows where they lay on the ground, the fathers and sons would walk together retracing their path back across the land to the pile of stones. They continued these journeys, each time taking another stone from the pile and setting off in a different direction from the pile itself, to discover the limits of their land. Whatever direction they took, they always arrived at the sea, and they always also found at the point where the land met the sea, a fortified tower with men in a hut at its top, who were deaf to the callings of the fathers. Of course, these journeys were exciting for the fathers and sons, because they never knew what each new day's journey would have in store for them, even though a predictable pattern of discovery eventually set in - the sea and men in a tower who wouldn't listen. And of course, the pile of stones got smaller and smaller, as each stone in its turn was carried and then used as a pillow and abandoned at a different limit of the fathers and son's good green land.

Now, during the days of all these journeys, the mothers were worked off their beautiful feet. Their charts and maps, with the plotting's of all these journeys, really began to take shape. There was no time for table tennis anymore. A picture of the green land of which they were queens was clearly forming. In a few days more, when the fathers and sons had journeyed out from the pile of stones in the remaining directions that needed to be taken to clinch the last limits of the land, the mothers would, with a bit of imagination, be able to join all the dots and the shape of their lovely land would be complete. This was exciting, but there was something else that was exciting as well. Something - though the mothers didn't know exactly what - was beginning to appear beneath the pile of stones, what with the pile growing smaller and smaller as the fathers and sons carried away new stones, as they began another of their journeys.

The mother's excitement wasn't confined to what was happening outside though. There were also odd rumblings from the cellar beneath.

Moles are very self-contained creatures. Especially moles that are bigger than one would normally tolerate. Especially moles that are as big as a full-grown pig. There had clearly been neglect on the part of the mothers as regards the welfare of the mole. This was gravely in evidence to the mothers when, on entering the cellar, the mole was nowhere to be seen.

There was a hole. But there was no... mole. A hole and the shape of the bulk of the mole forming a tunnel in the cellar wall with, when the mothers looked closely, no light to suggest an end to it. They were torn between, on the one hand, wanting to follow the mole, and on the other hand, wanting to finish the job with the charts and maps, to discover the complete shape of the land of which they were queens. There was also, whatever it was, gradually beginning to appear from beneath the pile of stones. The tunnel without light could wait, they thought. Let's do one job at a time. Complete one thing, before we start something else.

The fathers and sons could feel all at once that they were nearing the end of the biggest of all adventures. Each held a picture in his head of the shape of the land on which they all lived, but only some of them knew what a land of this shape was called. On what they all agreed would be their last journey out from the pile of stones, again, there was just the sea and a fortified tower on stilts at the edge of the land. As before, the fathers called out to the men that they could see moving about in the hut at the top of the tower. But this time, their calls did not fall upon deaf ears.

Together the twin sons were heard to shout, 'It's a flag, fathers. A flag on a pole. A white flag on a pole. See?' Sure enough, there was a white flag on a pole, being waved out of the hut at the top of the tower. 'Well! Bugger me.', said the fathers in unison, 'Bugger me'.

After a time of furious flag waving, a man opened a door at the back of the hut, the side of the hut that faced the sea. He climbed down a wooden staircase, that led from the hut to the ground beneath, where the fathers and sons were waiting patiently.

A black hood covered the man's face, though there were holes in it for his eyes and his mouth. One of his arms was held in a sling, and there was blood on the sling. What is all this, the fathers said. Tell us and our sons the story if you'd be so kind. And so, the man did. He told the captivated fathers and sons the story of his last twenty-five years. But, at the close of his story, they were none the wiser.

He said that at one time, way back, himself and all the other men in all the other huts had lived on the good green land where he, at last, now stood again. He said that things had been happy, but that over time, those same things had turned sour. That people whom he had at one time trusted, he'd grown to distrust. He wanted things for the land, and they wanted things for the land. But the things that were wanted were different. No agreements could be struck, so they fought for the land and the rights that they believed they each had. The fighting had, for a time, happened on the land itself, on the ground that the fathers and sons enjoyed their days upon. He said that some of the people then began to build towers so that they could get a better shot at the people that they didn't agree with. He said that eventually, each small group that believed a different thing, built a high tower for themselves, to get a better shot at those that believed something different. In time, everybody lived in a tower, and nobody lived on the land. And they fired shots at one another, from one tower to the other.

More and more people died. The towers were moved further and further apart, in the hope that so much unnecessary loss of life might be avoided. The towers were built higher each time and were moved further apart from one another until they all stood at the lands limit, where it met the sea. Then there was nowhere else to go.

He said that bullets crossed the sky for years and years, from one tower to the next. That many people died for the things that they believed in, and that others died not knowing what exactly it was that they believed in anymore.

He said that one day a white flag had appeared from an individual tower, but that all others had considered this a hoax and therefore continued with their firing bullets across the sky. He said that over the years, each individual tower had extended a white flag out for all others to see, but that nobody had ever believed that anybody else's intentions were honourable, and so things had continued on and on.

It occurred to the fathers to ask the man therefore, why he had, at long last, left his tower. And so, they did. They asked this very question. And the man replied, 'It's a funny thing, but do you know, this very day, that all white flags, from all the towers with the people believing different things, have appeared out in the sky together, and this including the tower of the people that I believe with. I haven't heard a shot in a while, have you? In fact, not since the lot of you arrived here. It's a strange world we live in, is it not? What I'll do now is return to my tower if you've got no objections. To watch and wait and hope for the best'. With that said, the hooded man turned from the fathers and sons, climbed the wooden staircase, and shut himself back into his hut on stilts. To watch and wait. And to hope for the best.

It became obvious that the sons were not overly impressed at what they saw as the conclusion to this biggest of all adventures. It just wasn't what they had been expecting. A man in a black hood telling them a story that maybe they would understand in years to come, but at the moment, what they wanted was stories of Unicorns or at the very least, stories about fantastic mothers. The walk back from this, their last journey to the limits of the land, was a silent and sad affair. Anxious fathers and long faced sons tramping on the good green land.

'It's an island on which we live', the fathers had proudly announced, when they finally arrived back at the now diminished pile of stones. This pile of stones from which they had begun each and every one of their journeys, that formed the biggest of all adventures. 'So what?!!', the sons all exclaimed in unison.

'It's an island.', said the mothers together, as they joined the last of the dots together on their maps and charts. 'It's an island, and the fathers and sons don't seem altogether happy, do they?'

On the other side of the big two-way mirror, two fathers and four sons were staring at themselves, each armed with a stone from the pile, a pile that wasn't really a pile anymore. It was more a mess of stones now. The fathers and sons had rifled the pile to find the biggest stones that they could. They'd disturbed the pile so much, that what had, at one time, been buried beneath it, was now almost fully revealed. It was a small boat, just big enough to carry two people, so the mothers decided, as they stared at it all beautifully excited.

The two mothers headed for the cellar, in the hope that their mole had found some light at the end of his tunnel.

The father with the stepson asks the stepson to stand back a little, to get a good footing and take aim. This could be an even better adventure than the biggest of all adventures think the fathers as they give the signal for the stone throwing to commence.

The mothers are in the tunnel now and they meet the mole coming towards them. 'You're going the wrong way', say the mothers to the mole. 'No, I'm not', says the mole to itself. 'Can you swim?' says the mole to itself but wishes that the mothers could hear.

There was a mirror oh so very beautiful, and then suddenly there isn't anymore. Heavy stones do such vicious damage to such delicate glass.

The fathers and sons can no longer see themselves. What they can see though, is a room, through the shattered and jagged shards of glass. They can see plenty of cheese and brandy and piled high boxes of candy. They can see charts and maps. They can see close up photographs of themselves with various faces, littering the floor of the room.

The two mothers are well into the tunnel now and they can see some light. But it's the light leaking from the hole in the bottom of the boat that the mole made, as it scratched and clawed its way out into the world of the fathers and sons.

Meanwhile, the mole fills in the hole in the cellar wall and listens with pleasure to the chatter and laughter of children as it re-joins its friends, the tortoise the lizard and the angel fish.

The boat is pushed aside by a mother's strong hands, and then both mothers are able to stand on the good green land at last, but not for long. They look back towards the building in which is their beautiful room. They see the fathers and sons drinking and eating of the brandy and candy. The mothers want to call out to them, but then what would the mothers say? Instead, they drag the boat together out across the land, out towards the sea. They follow the course of the last journey taken by the fathers and sons. They reach a limit to the land where this meets the sea and stop for a moment at the foot of a hut that is high up into the sky on stilts.

Everything is quiet.
Everything is still quiet.
They launch the boat into the sea.

The children have found the pets in the cellar and the fathers are playing table tennis together. 'This is great', say all the little sons to themselves, and they say this to the fathers as well. The sons wonder who it was that lived in this place, where they'd searched many times for a door, just a door. The fathers didn't have the heart to tell them the truth, but the fathers knew, and thought it better to say nothing, or else to make something up about a fantastic this or a fantastic that.

There's a hole in this boat, says one mother to the other. Trust a mole, to make a hole. 'Where shall we swim to?'

There are two mothers, and they are floating in the sea on their backs. They are chatting and both wondering what will happen next. They float and chat happily in this way for many days. For many months. For many years. Staring up at the sky.

We are getting through too many dreams. One day soon, we will run out. All around us are the broken shards of battles lost and the debris that is left behind after the celebration of hollow victories. We are constantly replacing one dream for another - we are getting through too many dreams. One day soon we will run out. Maybe we should stop looking for a new bright and shiny dream to dream. Maybe we should pick up the pieces of our shattered forgotten hopes and try to fit their useless fragments together to make our hollow victories whole.

This is the thought of the two mothers.

This is the thought of the two fathers.

This is the thought of the man with the hood from the hut on stilts in the sky.

It is also the thought of the mole.

I

I am embarrassed about having a small denture.

I am frightened of being on my own.

I have never told anyone about the failure of my anus two years ago. and how this has affected me.

I would like to be famous and am ashamed to admit to this.

I might be an alcoholic.

I own three and a half thousand books.

I can't   make   up my mind.

I am constantly putting things into my mouth.

My mother who is called Joan is bald.

I am obsessive about everything:

About my son,

about keeping things clean,

about making sure that my house will never be burgled,

about the length of my hair,

about the language that I use,

about saving money,

about not seeing my parents more than twice each year,

about my name,

about being different to the person that I probably should have been,

about being trusted and respected for being the person that I have become.

I like the smell of being bored.

People that are stupid say that I am very intolerant of them.

I believe it is important to be clear with stupid people, for the sake of the future.

I eat a large number of bananas each day, in the hope that this might stave off the ageing process.

Perhaps I am just being very naïve?

There is something about the word 'IDEA' that leaves me wondering at the end of each day.

I looked at a frog.

I noticed a bat.

I looked at some things in the world.

I saw a train.

I saw a bee.

I thought of a fly.

I noticed some things in the world.

I talked to a child.

I listened to a child.

I struggle to remember being a child.

I saw darkness and wondered about it.

I saw a light switched on in a room and noticed the difference that it makes.

I peeled a banana and ate it.

I smoked a cigarette and wondered why I'd done that.

I laughed and it surprised me.

I thought shit things about the world and my life, and this didn't surprise me.

I wondered about who else might have written about the things that I have written about here, in the way that I have written them.

I thought and I thought, and I thought and then I did something:

I went outside and I felt much better about being the person that I am.
I looked at the sun and I thought okay, if I need nothing else, I at least need this.

Once upon a time there were two people in a room, arguing about love.
About whether it really existed, or was just a nonsense, trumped up somewhere long ago to counter the fear of loneliness.

Noticing's

One
I notice a sixty-something Chinese man fishing, alone on the river Cam.
A simple pole, and a simple line, and a baked been sized can for bait.
Nothing else.
This man is perfectly okay.
With himself.
And the world that he is in.
Silent.
Still.
And serene.

He will catch fish, but he won't be bothered if he doesn't.

And if he doesn't?

He'll still go home and laugh.

Two
There is a pig in an urban front garden, loving every minute of its time there.

Three
Sometimes we are all foolish with time.

Four

A young boy wants to be Peter Pan, and truly believes that he can actually be this.

Five

Things that are broken are of little use and yet some of us keep them long after they break.

Six

Where are all of the people now that I used to know in the past?

Seven

What is the difference between something written by Jeffrey Archer and something scrawled on a pad late at night by my dead friend Laurence?

It is the difference between greed and pain probably.

Eight

I fumbled around with my dick in the dark, but that was okay, after all that had gone before.

Nine

In the USA, psychiatrists have Botox injected into their foreheads to prevent them from looking surprised.

Ten

I wish I had an angel of my own right now, to help me on my way.

Eleven

I saw a man, with two mobile phones. He had one at each ear. I thought, you must be terribly busy. I thought to myself, I'm glad I'm not as busy as you. Ho hum.

Twelve

Why are most houses not big enough for most people to live in?

Who decided that the average house would be such and such a size?

Thirteen

I saw a man with a loaf of bread on his head, doing his general shopping, as if this was nothing out of the ordinary.

He didn't look in the slightest bit awkward, or embarrassed, and so I suppose it was indeed nothing out of the ordinary for him.

Good for him, I thought.

Fourteen

Why do other peoples' trades, always seem infinitely more interesting than my own trade?

Fifteen

I heard a woman say today:

'Like most men, he has selective hearing'.

What am I to make of such a thing?

Sixteen

My son said to me today.

'Last night, when I did a pee, I managed to pee all down my leg.

I must have a puncture in my willy, somewhere, don't you think Dad?'

I wasn't sure how to answer, but I did reassure him that all was not lost.

At least, I hope I did.

Seventeen
Some scientists, for example, call the Earth, the Goldilocks planet, because Venus,

hot enough to melt lead, was too warm and Mars, the frozen desert, was too cold,

but Earth was just right for life.

Eighteen
Lots of people, fat or thin, cycle to school during a crisis. Why, only during a crisis, do they do this I wonder?

Nineteen
The one thing that I have noticed is that it doesn't rain, but it pours.

Twenty
I have come to notice that security guards think that they are policemen these days.

Twenty-One
I have also noticed that the Police act like security guards these days.

Twenty-Two
I have noticed, that so many people don't stay nice and calm for very long these days.

Twenty-Three

I have also noticed that so many people in my class lose house points, more than they gain them.

Fathers Can Be

I

Fathers can be seed, just seed, and then away running, walking, or by car in the night, until the next time.

Some fathers know well that this is who they are, and some fathers don't, until the phone rings, or the letter arrives.

Some fathers are bottled, and membership is not required. These are the smallest of all fathers and are not easily recognised in the street.

Seed and away in the night forever after fathers are small but have less credibility than the smallest of all fathers.

Some fathers seed and stay and are lousy because they know they should have left earlier, and guilt begins to rot them.

Some seed and stay fathers do the best that they can, but this tends to cause a great deal of shouting - particularly at night, when they, the fathers, need to sleep.

Some fathers seed and then lose it on purpose at the hospital after much deliberation.

Some fathers don't want to seed, not yet anyway, but do, and are jolly good.

Some fathers want to seed, but can't, and promptly go out to buy a dog or a new car, or a gadget of some kind.

Some fathers want to seed, have always wanted to, do, and are jolly good, and they and their partners have a fine old time of it.

Some fathers seed and then the mother gets hit by a train, or her drinking habit gets the better of her liver and the single parent father is born. These fathers are rarely seen. They are like Pandas, but not as distinctively marked.

Fathers are all sorts, and are seeded differently according to ability, common sense, initiative, willingness to learn, and earning capacity.

II

Will I do it right? Will I be there? Will I turn a blind eye when I shouldn't see? Will I love as necessary? Will I be dangerous, exciting, stern, useful, engaging, funny, healthy? Will I understand and be understood? Will I panic? Will I listen? Will I shout, and if I do, what will this feel like? Will I be any good at tennis, cricket, and football when I'm sixty? Will I be of use to you? I hope so. I very much hope so.

III

A child is in a colourful sun filled garden, standing, head pitched back, eyes wide, searching the sky. What is this child thinking?

A child jams its fingers in the space between a closing door and door frame. It looks at its own trembling hand, the skin all torn and rearranged. It feels its own tears falling into its mouth. What is this child thinking?

A child watches a cow giving birth to a calf in a field. Then it watches the calf leave its mothers side almost at once, like a callipered cripple. What is this child thinking?

A child sees a cartoon cat and dog arguing the toss. Then it sees the dog behind the wheel of a steam roller. It sees the steam roller engulf the cat. It sees the flat cat and the smug dog. It sees the dog drive the steam roller into the path of an express train that suddenly appears from nowhere. It sees the cat reflate manually to its former shape, sees the cat looking oh so smug in its turn. What is this child thinking as it laughs?

A child catches its parents urgently fucking, trying to find the love inside one another, all partially clothed, up against the fridge in the kitchen. What is this child thinking about the pleasure that can exist between two people?

In a casual television house, a child witnesses one human being execute another with a bullet through the temple. What is this child thinking about human dignity?

In a carefully prepared garden, a child tramples vegetables and coloured flowers back into the earth to retrieve its comforter blown away in the wind. What is this child thinking?

A child watches a house burn to the ground. The house next door. When the fire is done, the child continues to help its toy elephant and clown dance together on the back lawn. What is this child thinking about the responsibility of owning property?

A child is blind and deaf from birth. What is this child thinking about all possible worlds?

In a child's bedroom, there are fossils of its parents and grandparents set into opposite walls. What must the future of this child be?

IV

What will you remember, if I remember this?:

I remember, aged eight or nine, visiting the toilet in our house - an urgent visit. I remember tangled trousers on the floor at my feet. Then looking down into the bowl through the gap between my legs. I remember the blackbird there, in the water, drowned between my legs, its yellow beak breaking the surface like a periscope. I remember my heart thundering at the shock. This shouldn't be here; it should be in its nest. Had it dropped there from inside of me? What had I eaten to warrant this? 'There's a blackbird drowned in the toilet', was the cry. 'It's only a blackbird. Why all this fuss young man', was the soothing voice from the other side of the door. 'But it should be in its nest though, or it should be in the sky.'

What will you remember if I remember this?:

I remember a crowded station platform, and the rain in sheets.

I remember a group of skinheads - going on holiday, they were.

And a wino in a broken Parker, the Parkers stuffing pouring out into the light.

I remember the skinheads surrounding the Parker and the man in it, and all their laughter at his smell and rotten teeth. I remember the skinhead Spike, whose face changed suddenly into the position for spitting, for gobbing heavily with his slippery shot.

Spike spat on the man with the smell and rotten teeth. Then him and his holiday chums spat at the man together, who didn't move. Spit and gob like the sheets of rain fell on the man.

On his hair.

On his clothes.

On his face and hands.

He didn't move, and everybody watched the shame filling his face.

I was much too small to step in, but there were others there who weren't, but didn't - including my father.

A shamed man covered in skinhead spit from head to toe is what I remember, and then the train arrived, and the skinheads went on their holidays, leaving their spit behind them.

What will you remember if I remember this?:

I remember games under the sheets with my sisters. I remember games under the sheets with myself. I remember that these games with myself involved socks and wads of tissue and canisters of talcum powder. Talcum powder for the benefit of my parents' nostrils, whom I was convinced could smell the rat in these games with myself and that if they did, I'd have to come clean and explain myself, for playing with myself.

V

Dr Mengele was making the selections.

He stood there tall, nice looking, and he was dressed very well, as if he wanted to make a good impression.

He had very soft hands, and he made fast decisions.

His secretary would measure the children, while Mengele examined them.

He was especially interested in their hair.

He would look closely at the roots, to see how it was growing.

It is said by some that Joseph Mengele loved children - even though he was a murderer and a killer.

Yes, it is said by some that Joseph Mengele was:

A 'gentleman'.

Simon And Bob

Saturday. Five o'clock - a.m:

I've got the biscuit tin for collecting all the people's money in, so now everything is ready for the huge day that is today. It's a good tin. A great one. A big one. A Peak Freens five-decker. The last bicky went just now. Into my mouth. Every night, ten bickies into my mouth. Under the sheets. All dark. Crunching away for an empty tin, without them upstairs even knowing a jot of it. Good tastes in the dark. And in the mornings, crumbs, and some of those very pretty folded paper biscuit cups for screwing up and hiding away in the drawer under the hankies and pants and socks, so that them upstairs won't notice, and ask all the difficult questions.

When it comes to me and what I do, they've both got great big noses that they like to push around inside my head. It makes me cry a lot - sometimes. So, I do all of the things that they would nose about, well, I do them in the dark, where their noses can't get. Like the business with the biscuits and other things as well.

I'm good in the dark now, but it wasn't always like that. At first, when they forced me out of the day, I had to do everything very slowly, and even then, I still got the nasty bruises from the table corners and precious things got broken. Little hills of purple and yellow pain on my ginger leg-tops, but even these were still better than all the silly questions.

There are some things though that I can do which are just really okay with them, because of who I am and the label that some other people who are very important say I need, so that they, my mum and dad, get that extra money which makes me all the more worthwhile. Yes. That's what they say.

So, when my legs started to hurt really too much, I pushed everything in my room up against the walls. Really tight against the skirting boards. They make me laugh. Skirting boards. Just the name of them. I rolled the carpet up as well and this went where everything else went. Up against the.......I can't say it again because it's too funny. Yes. Go on. Go on. Up against the skirting boards. What a laugh. Who invented them, and why are they in some rooms and not others? That's a great question, that one is. I have a friend whose house doesn't have any skirting boards, but I haven't told him, so he's all ignorant about them.

Moving things around in my room like this is fine for everyone because it is part of what my label means. It's good to know that this kind of thing is off limit for noses.

It is five o'clock in the morning and I'm waiting for the light, sitting tight against the window in my room. Looking out at nothing and thinking great thoughts about what a huge day today will be. The two of them are still upstairs sleeping, when they should be up and about making my sandwiches and diluting some orange juice. I learned that word yesterday. Diluting. But I can't remember where it happened. That's mostly how it is with words though. Once you get the basic hang of them, new ones just keep sticking to you like honey on your fingers, bubble gum on your shoe, or like those green grassy flea darts in the summer that really like living on my jumpers, particularly when they are thrown there by somebody who has just finished, or is in the middle, of laughing at me.

Five o'clock and dark, and all the nonsense movements of this house being heard by my ears. The turning over grumbles of my mum and dad upstairs, getting those great pictures in their heads of the three of us in heaven riding around in a big ship on the sea, going wherever I want to, and eating whatever I please.

I really do like the sea and everything in it, but we had to move away from places where it was near, because I kept walking into it and nearly drowning. Extra lines appeared on my mum's face and grey hair sprouting like a fountain from her head after the sea had nearly taken me away for perhaps the twelfth or thirteenth time.

There's only the sea in books now though, and plus in my dreams of heaven. I know how deep the oceans are which is very exciting, and I have some coral and shells and stones on the table by my bed which are all lovely. God says that he made the heaven and the earth, including the sea, and I believe him.

There's the milkman coming up the path. He walks around in the dark like everyone else does in the day. Just because he's used to the dark I suppose, and maybe because his bright white coat helps him to see a little better than we all can. I really don't know about that, but I don't want to be a milkman anyway, so there's no point in thinking about it for longer than that first thought that I just had. The milkman's got his money bag with him, but I hope he doesn't start banging our door, because if he does, there could be trouble in store for him, since my dad is huge, and hates being woken up at five o'clock in the morning. I know this because I have done it to my dad myself at five o'clock and earlier, and this is when he punches me the hardest of all, as well as calling me little ginger fucker. But being small and ginger isn't bad, is it?

One time, at three o'clock, when I was climbing out of the sash window in my room and when I knocked a table over with a clumsy foot, he woke up. He ran into my room, with his hair all over the place, and jammed the sash window down on my fingers, breaking my two favourite ones. I was on the outside of our house, hanging from my room sash window-ledge. I fell into the roses with my two favourite fingers broken, and he then came outside and dragged me really hurting back in through the front door, and that was when he punched me the hardest of all right on the nose, and I went straight to heaven that time and no mistake.

In the day, my dad is different. When my mum is there. But in the night, he is a monster with many changing heads. In the day, he rushes to the shops to buy me things, saying that what happened in the night is, our little secret, and because he gets me what I want in the day, I believe him and say nothing about the night time, apart from to say to my mum and other people that ask, that I fell over hitting my face on the sink in the bathroom, or that a door blew closed from a big draught and I forgot to take my fingers away in time. They have sad looks on their faces when I tell them these things, and I'm certain they're thinking, poor little ginger twerp. But I think it's a long time until heaven comes, and a person shouldn't take everything to heart, should they?

My dad gets me the things that I want and that is why today will happen as it will. I've been thinking about it now for months and months. Where to do it. How to do it. And of course, all the things that it will bring when I've done it. Like a great deal of money. Interviews on the TV with other famous people. T- Shirts with my ginger face on them, smiling out at the world all rich and famous like not many people are. It is a great life, isn't it? Yes. No question about that.

Saturday. Six o'clock - a.m:

The light is in my room now. Six o'clock. Saturday - a.m. Only four hours to go before I hit what my dad calls, 'The Headlines'.

Naked in front of my bedroom mirror.

Me.

This is the body of a star.

Yes, it is.

How many ginger stars are there? Not many and that's a fact.

I look at myself. I have the voices of mum and dad in my head, and the voices of those people at the swimming pool where I go to hang around in the water and have a great laugh splashing and taking a good look at some of the girls and ladies and the very great treasures that they hold inside their swimming things. I think that tits are wonderful, even though I've never touched even one. All these voices saying so many things about me. Painfully Thin, Ginger Flamingo, Trumpet Face. Well, they will laugh on the other side of their own faces when they read the headlines tomorrow morning. You bet your life they will. They'll be wanting to show me their tits then. Oh yes. They certainly will. And I will love them all. Every one of them. My fans. I look great without my clothes on. And nothing like a blimmin flamingo.

There are stirrings upstairs now. The alarm clocks gone off at two hours past the time that we agreed it would. They must have forgotten, I suppose. Yes. That must be it.

I can cut all the price tickets off of my costume now, because they said I could today. I've been very good about it. New trousers, shirt, socks, jacket, shoes, all in the dark of my wardrobe since last Saturday, and I've only got them out to look at three or four times a day every day since then. Mum says that's very good for me with new things, and the waiting so long to cut the price tickets off is a real breakthrough and she's sure that everybody who needs to know will be very impressed. Well done, Simon. Yes. Well done me.

Saturday. Eight o'clock - a.m:

It's breakfast now with mum and dad and a huge mountain of cereal, because I tipped the packet up too much, and it just all fell out into my bowl. I must be very careful about the milk and jam and stuff and keeping it all off my shirt and jacket and socks and trousers and shoes. A little bit does get on, but I'm sure it won't show when all the people are looking at me later, because it's going to be very sunny, and there will be so much else going on what with them all swinging away, that I doubt it'll notice.

As usual, breakfast is a quiet time. I knock things over now and again and make a mess, but that's how it always is. Apart from dad huffing and puffing, we're not saying anything.

I've asked for lettuce, tomato and cheese sandwiches and the biggest bottle of diluted squash that's on earth for my lunch, and mum says that that is no problem. She makes it all for me and its done.

Saturday. Nine thirty o'clock - a.m:

Half past nine and time to go. Dad has made me wait until just before I go out of the door. He says, 'Go and get your bag Simon, and while you're doing that, I'll get the other things that we talked about.' He thinks that I don't know that he's got what I asked for, but I do. Because when he was out on Tuesday, I used my torch and shined it through the gap between the locked doors of his wardrobe, and there were my other things all ready and waiting.

I run upstairs to my room, hide the Peak Freens tin in the bottom of my bag, and I'm halfway down the stairs again before he is even halfway up. Then I wait with the front door half open. After a long time, with rummaging sounds from his room, he then comes down with all the things that I asked for. They're great. Really new and good. The guitar. The Walk-Man. The Bob Dylan tape - my friend without any skirting boards in his house says that Bob Dylan is great, and my friend is not usually wrong. And there's that baseball cap that I asked for with the really long peak on it. Wow to that as well.

Dad hands everything over now, with half a smile stretched across his fat face. I know that he's thinking, Ginger Twerp, Ginger Flamingo, but he'll want some of it when I make all the money won't he? I don't know where mum is, but she doesn't say goodbye, so maybe she's on the telephone or something.

Here I go then. Front door pushed closed against my back. My own legs to take me along the road into town. Past the rest of the even numbers in my road. Then a little gap and past the front of the football stadium. Then a much bigger gap. A nice small field and then the great little church that is always shut. Hey. No, it's not. Not today. The great big door is open and there is time to look inside if I'm quick. Ten o'clock is fifteen minutes away and I'm only five minutes from town now.

There are awkward steps down to the church, but I manage to do everything right for a change, because I concentrate very hard and don't get distracted by the traffic or birds in the sky, or a thought about something very different coming into my head.

There are two people in the church, but not one of them has the special clothes on. They're moving chairs and tables about like I do in my room at home. God isn't actually here with them at this time, but I can feel him saying hello to me and welcome.

There are some things I need to know from the two people, so I just ask them the way I always do.

'Do you live here?' I say.

'No', they say together.

'How much does it cost to live here?' I say.

'We don't live here, nobody does', they say.

'When I make all the money today, I will buy this church and live here with you', I say.

‘Yes’, they say. ‘Okay’, they say. ‘Look’, they say. ‘We really are rather busy right now’, they say.

‘Moving in, or moving out?’ I say. ‘Can I drive your van?’ I say.

One of them is a woman and one of them is a man. The man laughs under his breath. At me. And the woman gives him a really nasty look like she might want to punch him hard.

‘Look, please, we’re really busy’, she says. ‘Honestly!’ she says.

Whilst she’s saying this, he’s looking at me thinking.......I know exactly what he’s thinking. He’s thinking, You stupid ginger flamingo. Go away. I do not speak ginger flamingo, and even if I did, I wouldn’t be speaking to you.

When people are like this with me, I sometimes choose to hang around for just that little bit too long, shutting out any more words from me, in the hope that the people will feel very awkward. So, this is what I do for two minutes more. I check my watch and it is a very long and awkward two minutes for the man. Serves him right. Then I leave. I say goodbye to the woman, not because she is much nicer than the man when all is said and done, but because she has a tight top on and her tits look like they’re good.

I get away from the church and leave these two Christians to their devices. Up the awkward steps again. Trip over slightly, but nothing gets broken, and I carry on walking into town. Over the railway bridge with no trains to be seen anywhere. The sun is really bright now. I’m glad I’ve got my hat. I chose the right one for the day. That’s a good sign.

Shops now. A tiny bakery. A doughnut would be great, but nah, maybe not. A flower shop with some great colours everywhere. I think I like being alive on days like this when I’ve got butterflies inside, and I’m thinking a lot about all the money and fame not far off.

Into town properly now, through under where its covered, where Boots store sells everything but boots, and into the market square. My stadium.

There are loads of people walking around already, waiting for me to start. Yes. That's exactly what they're up to. They've got tons of shopping and its only just ten o'clock.

Saturday. Ten o'clock - a.m:

I set all my gear up. The biscuit tin in front for all the people's money. Put Bobs tape carefully into the Walk-Man and put the headset over my cap and into my ears. Squat down cross legged on the ground and put the guitar in my lap like a real professional. I've really got the butterflies now.

The crowd of people walking around with all their things looks really huge now. Especially because I'm sitting down on the ground and looking up at them all. People are careful about their shopping and about looking at me. Very few of them do - look at me that is.

It's time to start, before I lose them. I press play and there's Bob inside my head between my ears. He's great. He really is. Wait for the money now to start rolling into my tin.

Sitting there like I am, I don't play my guitar. Not one strum. Because what Bob does on his is much better. I don't sing a note either with my own voice, because Bobs is great on its own, isn't it? And I don't move at all, because this might put Bob off of what he is doing, inside my head between my ears.

When he finishes a song, all I do is tap my tin very quietly with one of my ginger fingers and stop doing this as soon as he starts again. He's a legend my friend says, and I want to be just like him.

Doing it like I do means that I can eat my sandwiches and drink my drink without having to stop anything. Bob just goes on inside my head.

There's a special button on my Walk-Man which means that both sides of the tape play one after the other, so I don't have to ever turn the tape over. I just have to press play again when both sides are finished one time through.

I notice people's faces haven't changed though. Not even for Bob Dylan inside my head. There's just the same thinking going on, but there are many more of them than just my dad or people like those two at the church. You know what they're thinking don't you?

Stupid Ginger Twerp.

Stupid Ginger Flamingo.

Poor Sad Little Fucker.

Some people like it though. They like me and Bob inside my head being a legend. They have the sweetest of smiles for both of us, sweet sad and sorry smiles, and they put the smallest of their small change in my tin.

Eleven o'clock. Twenty-four pence.

Twelve o'clock. Twenty-six pence.

One o'clock. Thirty-six pence.

Two o'clock. Forty pence.

Three o'clock. Forty-two pence. Run out of sandwiches. Run out of drink.

Five o'clock. Fifty pence, but it looks a lot more because it's all in ones and twos.

Six o'clock. Fifty pence and a button. A man with bad eyesight threw the wrong thing.

Six minutes passed six o'clock. The batteries have gone in my Walk-Man, and so has Bob inside my head for real, but I can imagine him carrying on, and so that is what I'll do.

Seven o'clock. No more people and a really long shadow of me across the cobbled market square.

I think it's the end.
The end of today for now.
My butterflies have turned to moths.

It was a huge day. But I know it was so huge only for me.
Not for anyone else.
Maybe, when dad hits me again, I could ask him to get me a model aeroplane, and then I could be a great pilot like Douglas Barder.

No, perhaps not, eh?

Stupid Ginger Flamingo.
Stupid Ginger Twerp.

Not As It Is Now

She has a four wheeled pushchair that has one of its wheels missing. But this pushchair never carries a child. I see it pushed, by her, back and forth, just across the road from my house in the village. See her, through a handy crack that parts the bedroom curtains, through the frosted pane of the front door window, when I pull my eye close enough to the glass. Which I do. Whenever Vera travels by.

I see her behind me, with all her purpose, from the interior mirror of my car. You see, sometimes I invent things to be doing in the car, parked on its driveway, its arse poking out into the road, when I know that Vera is out and about.

I first noticed her in January. That was when it started. Vera pushing her three wheels up and down the tar macadam paths. It wasn't every day. Not at first. At least I didn't realise that she made this journey every day. That took a while to come to the surface. Our patterns were different at first you see. One person, Vera, doing the same thing in exactly the same way at the same time every day, but at the start I wasn't always there to see her, so I wasn't to know that she was so regular.

It took time for me to arrange myself so that I could fall into sync with her. To be at home. By a door or a window. On the driveway in the car. In the front garden, fiddling with a tree or plant that in fact needed no attention at all. All this rearranging for the sake of Vera.

Looking back on it all now, my efforts to coincide with Vera's journeys seem ludicrous, but at the time it all made complete sense.

January 1995. The first sighting. A lip splitting wind roaring through the village and evidence of a heavy frost covering the garden, the road, the paths, and all. Me, in the car, trying to coax it to do what its designed to do. But it won't do it. It won't move. Were stuck, my car and me, on the frosted driveway, like a pair of lovers arguing together in the cold. Me getting very angry with a knackered old heap of French rubbish but going absolutely nowhere. I wonder if anybody is watching. I swivel the interior mirror on its mounting through many angles searching for laughing witnesses to me and my fallen Renault. There's nobody laughing, but there's a woman smiling.

A smiling woman pushing a crooked pushchair comes into view. I find myself following her journey in the mirror without at first quite knowing why. Then it dawns on me what the problem is. There is no sensible connection between what this woman is wearing and the temperature outside. She is bare legged. For a start. Loose fitting black canvas slip-on summer pumps almost hanging from her feet, the backs of them trodden and broken. A thin pastel coloured cotton summer dress that is short, almost to the point of itself being pointless. Like the canvas pumps, the cotton dress is also loose fitting, particularly in the region of the woman's breasts which are partially exposed. She is smiling at the distance. A wide and gaping fixed smile. Her bare arms and legs look badly bruised, though it may be that they're just suffering in colour from the cold.

She's locked into a July or August that disappeared into the winter months ago. And now she's opposite my house. Standing very still, there on the path, smiling like an idiot. She stands there for five minutes, ten minutes, and then half an hour has passed. Half an hour during which only the expression on her face changes. I know this because I watch her face change its expression minute by minute. From a gaping fixed idiotic smile, fraction by fraction, her face falls to no smile at all. And then, from no smile at all, again fraction by fraction, her face crawls into the position for crying. And then there are tears pulsing from her eyes. When the tears appear, she lets go of the pushchair, and walks onto the grass verge between the path and the road.

She looks to her right. She looks to her left. She looks to her right again. The tears are winding down across her face. I just carry on watching. Because I'm sealed inside the car, what she is doing seems more like something in a film, more this, than something that is actually happening just across the road from me. I should get out and say something or do something to help her, but I don't. I can't. I'm all white knuckles on the steering wheel. She stands on the verge.

The grass is still brittle with frost. She carries on crying and then, without what seems like a second thought, she takes violent hold of the hem of the cotton dress and pulls the whole thing up and over her head. There is suddenly a naked woman framed in the interior mirror of my car. She just stands there on the grass verge, her dress discarded on the ground beside her. There is a moment like this, and then another and then, with great care and precision, she lays her body down on the verge. Lays down on her back, positioning her head and all her limbs very carefully out across the verge, almost as if she is trying to recreate the position of a particular body in a painting. Her tears gradually subside, whilst she is shifting her body into what seems like a pre-set and very exact position on the verge.

She doesn't wince from the cold of the ground against her back. There is no concern about comfort it seems. The exactness of her position seems to be all that is important. The index finger of her left hand is the last detail of her body to arrive at its position of rest. Then, she simply closes her eyes. I can see her stomach rising and falling as she breathes. I notice that my knuckles aren't white on the steering wheel of the car any longer, and then I notice that I'm crying. Crying as I watch her lying there, not on film, but just across the road from my house.

I am more confused now than ever, and I still do nothing except watch. She lays there, eyes closed, for about two minutes, and then very casually, she just sits up, and then stands up. Picks up her dress. Slips it back on to cover her body. Takes hold of the pushchair again, turns it around, and then pushes it back along the path in the direction from which she had earlier come. All of these actions are undertaken as if nothing has happened at all over the previous half an hour or so.

I watch her disappear from the interior mirror of my car. Then I just sit there staring into the mirror. Seeing only the path, the verge, part of the road and part of the house that is directly opposite my own.

I get out of the car. I go back inside the house, and I think very hard about what it is that I have just seen.

At exactly the same time of day the next time after that that I am at home, about two weeks later, the same thing happens again. This time I am in my son's bedroom, tidying up, when through his bedroom window, Vera comes into view. Exactly as before, she does everything that she'd done on that first occasion. There is no discernible difference in the sequence from before. Now, of course, I am watching it all from a different perspective this time, but I know that she does it all exactly as before. Except....Except this time, as she is pushing the three wheeled pushchair back along the path in the direction from which she comes. From which she comes after the smiling, the tears, the laying down of her naked body, that final adjustment of the left-hand index finger and the closing of her eyes, she stops on the path, still holding the pushchair, turns her head and looks directly up at me watching her from behind my son's bedroom window.

Her face suddenly tightens, full of hatred and accusation. Her mouth opens and the words, 'It was someone just like you', scream out at me. She screams this same set of words three times, aiming all of them at me. Then she just turns away from me, carries on walking, and disappears from view.

I sit on the floor of my son's room, not crying this time, but feeling a sense of guilt that I can't find a home for.

Through February and March, I rearranged things so that I could be at home each day to witness Vera's time across from my house. I came to call her Vera because she reminded me vaguely of one of my father's sisters who was given that name.

It got to being every day that I watched Vera, though after that second occasion when she'd screamed out at me, I made sure that though I could see her, she wouldn't be able to see me.

She appeared every day and did exactly as she'd done on that first day. I watched and watched and watched. For a long time, I didn't see Vera out and about in the village at any other time other than during Vera's special time.

I knew nothing about her other than what I saw her do across the road from my house. She always looked exactly the same during her special time. Always wore the same clothes. The same shoes.

Then one day, having watched her as usual - arrive, do what she always did and then go - about half an hour later, there was a knock at my front door. I pulled the door open and there was Vera standing about a foot away from me.

She had her arms full and her pushchair full of vegetables - vegetables from my garden. I'd grown more than I'd needed you see, so I'd put the surplus out in front of the driveway in boxes with a cardboard sign asking people to please take them free of charge if they could use them. This was obviously what Vera had done, which was fine, but what I couldn't understand was why she felt she needed to call at the house as well.

We both stood there whilst I waited for her to say whatever it was that she wanted to say. I noticed that she was wearing lipstick - this was never the case during the times that I watched her. She looked at me very intensely, her eyes darting around as if she was trying to work something out, though I couldn't imagine what that might be.

I'd only ever heard her scream words before, but standing there just in front of me, she opened her red mouth moving her lips up and down, and a voice came out from between these that I couldn't connect at all with this woman in front of me. She said, without seeming to pause for breath:

'Are you sure, really sure, you see I don't usually do things like this, not without paying a small something at least, a little for you and your family, I do have money, but as you can see not on me at this moment, my children will be so pleased, something fresh from the ground, they will love it, the smells of these things all cooking in the kitchen and then all of us eating together like we always do, once a week at least I like to give them something fresh, but I don't have the ground the fingers or the patience to bring things like this into the world myself, not as good as these certainly, they are beautiful.

I wanted to say thank you, rather than just to walk away and say nothing, this is sometimes what happens with people, they just do silly things, strange things, serious things, dangerous things, horrible things, and then walk away leaving everybody to wonder about what they meant by this or that action, and everything turns itself on its head at times like these, you do understand what I mean of course because yes, of course you do, I can see everything written all over you that you understand, you've seen everything else about me as well, I know this because I've seen you looking from here over to there where it is that everything happens for me, it must seem very strange I'm sure, but believe me it's very important that it all happens exactly the way that it does, I did scream at somebody one day, maybe it was you, if it was I'm so sorry because of course it couldn't possibly be you, someone yes certainly, but not you certainly, someone much older perhaps and someone very strong, no that's not a polite joke, I'm being very serious, what do you make of what you see I wonder, something, nothing, anything, you don't have to say now, please it's alright, nothing will change, but then maybe someone, not you, but someone will see me there and remember what it was all about when things were very different here, yes, someone might have seen, might actually have seen her when they see me like you do and remember everything about it, I really hope that this can happen, because I can only see her when I think about it you see, and thank you again for the lovely vegetables, I'll let you know how everything goes with them and pass on the scores from the children, I must go, really, it's time I was going, they'll wonder where I am and that's never a good thing is it.'

I was just about to open my mouth and say I don't know what, but something, when Vera turned around, then walked down the drive, and then off with her pushchair and vegetables down the road.

I thought about what she'd said. I stood on the front doorstep, staring at her disappearing into the distance. As I was closing the front door, I happened to glance down and there on the ground in front of the doorstep was a black slip-on canvas pump identical in design to the ones that Vera wore during her special time, but different in as much that this single pump was a much smaller version. A scaled-down version that would fit a child. A small child aged five or six perhaps. I took the shoe back into the house with me, thinking that when Vera appeared for her time tomorrow, I could return it to her, since it had obviously fallen from the pushchair during her visit and our chat.

When tomorrow came though, Vera didn't appear. For the first time in all the months that I'd watched her, she didn't show up. A week went by. A fortnight. A month. No Vera. Things had changed. Something had happened.

The village that I live in isn't large. I guess that there are one hundred and fifty to two hundred houses in all. There are lots of lanes though that glue the village loosely together, just a few houses dotted about on each one. The spread of the village was one of the things that attracted me to it most of all. I'd moved here with my son three days before Christmas, the Christmas just a few weeks after which I'd first seen Vera.

It occurred to me that I'd been watching this woman for the last six months or so. But what about the people opposite in the house directly across from mine. What about the people in the three or four other houses that Vera would be able to see and would therefore be seen by, during her special time? Did they watch as well, and if they did, what did they think?

In fact, who were these other people? It dawned on me that though I'd been here for over six months, I didn't know the names of anyone else in this village that I was so fond of. I tried to conjure for myself the features of the people in the house opposite, but even this was difficult, and the features just kept shifting around inside my head.

When I'd first come here with my son to look at the house, we'd both walked all around the village, up and down all the little lanes, peering into gardens and houses, through hedgerows, just to get a feel of the place, which we decided afterwards felt good. This exploration though only happened once. We didn't do it again once we'd moved here. People don't though, do they? Or is it just me? I and perhaps they, get into a car and drive somewhere else to walk, to shop, to see friends. The place where we live, its detail, is unknown to most of us.

I had a child's shoe that didn't belong to me. It belonged to Vera. Vera, whoever she actually was, had appeared, and then disappeared just as suddenly. I didn't know for certain whether anyone else in the village saw Vera on a daily basis lie naked out on the verge across from my house. I didn't know why she did this. I didn't know where she came from. I knew details about certain aspects of her clothing and about certain aspects of her body. And I knew these details from a distance through various glass windows in my house, through the mirrors in my car, through the leaf spread of various large plants in my front garden. I knew some of the same things and some other things at a closer range because of our chat on my front doorstep.

The next weekend that I knew my son was due to be with his mother, I decided that I would attempt to find Vera. I decided that I'd do again, but this time on my own, what my son and I had done when we'd first looked around the village together before moving here.

I walked all the lanes of the village, to see if I could find Vera, although I didn't know exactly what I would do if in fact I did find her. It was a ridiculous thing to be doing I know, but to me, it did seem to make sense.

I wandered around, up and down lanes that I'd almost forgotten existed. I peered into gardens, into houses, through hedgerows, desperately trying to find a woman who I knew virtually nothing about. I wasn't even certain that she actually lived in the village.

I wandered around like this for two or three hours, working my way slowly past about fifty or sixty houses, and then I suddenly came across something that I recognised. My handwriting. On a cardboard sign. The sign said, 'Please feel free to take any of these if you can use them'. The sign was hanging from the handlebars of Vera's three wheeled pushchair that was standing at the entrance to a garden.

In the pushchair itself - and this may seem a strange thing to say but it's true - were all of the vegetables that had previously been stacked up in boxes outside of my own house. Even though they were now in various stages of acute decay, the quantities and variety of vegetables in Vera's pushchair matched almost exactly those of the vegetables that I'd placed outside my house about a month previously. Vera had obviously decided to re-let my vegetables for some reason, and then simply let them rot where they were stacked. In her pushchair.

Looking over the low stone wall into the garden, I could just about make out the outline of a cottage set fifty yards or so from where I was standing. The garden itself was a mass of overcrowded trees and vines and wild roses that had been left to do what they please. A bit like my vegetables really. How could she. Bitch.

I decided that this must be where Vera lived, and that if nothing else, I wanted to have the opportunity to tell her what I thought of the way in which she'd treated my vegetables. We all think strange things at odd times, don't we? I'd come here to hopefully resolve something else, but, as I stood there looking at my produce seeping and sweating with rot, the actual purpose of my visit there got temporarily second placed to the outrage that I felt looking at this mouldy vegetable hill.

I forced open a broken wooden gate that was almost set rigid into a gap in the low stone wall and then I walked up a tatty little grass engulfed crazy paving path towards the cottage. When I got to the cottage itself, the front door was open. I noticed on the wall just inside the open door that Vera's pastel coloured cotton dress was suspended from it on a wooden hanger. On a stone tiled floor beneath the dress were Vera's black canvas pumps, both of them, and just next to these was the smaller child's version. Just the one. Not a pair.

When I saw the dress and the shoes, little edited snap shots of Vera across from my house started flying at tangents around inside my head. I reached into one of my pockets and pulled out the lost shoe that I'd brought with me.

It was also at this point that a heap of questions occurred to me. What did I want to know? Why did I want to know? Did I have a right to know? Would she tell me anything? Would I make a fool of myself? What would I do with whatever it was that she told me, if of course she told me anything? Was I just a nosy bastard who had gained a perverse pleasure from peeping on a naked woman who just happened to choose to be naked just across the road from where I live? Why the fuck didn't I just stop looking, stop making such an effort to look? Was I unusual in that I saw and then wanted to carry on seeing to the point eventually of not wanting to be seen seeing? What was the right and the wrong here? Questions like these, with me standing outside Vera's front door. The conscience monster hard at work, crawling out of its dark cave when the time is right, or wrong, depending upon how you look at it.

I wanted to know what the fuck had gone on, in order to know why the fuck what went on went on, and then I might discover, or be able to think through to what might happen in the future. It was all just one big fucking tangent at that moment.

I bent down and put the little child's shoe back in its place, completing the second pair, there beneath the pastel-coloured cotton dress. I called out the words, Excuse me, loudly, aiming these into the cottage. I called out half a dozen times but there was no answer. I walked into the hall of the cottage. An awkward, hesitant trying to be nonchalant walk. I couldn't hear anybody moving about in the house, apart from me that is.

The hall extended about thirty feet, leading to another open door, where the kitchen was. There was a stairwell set into the wall just before the entrance to the kitchen and four other doors, two on either side of the hall. All of these doors were slightly open. I walked to the door that was closest to me. I knocked on it gently, calling out, 'Excuse me', but again there was no answer. I pushed this door fully open so that I could see further into the room itself.

The floor of the room had stripped and polished floorboards and there were five small circular rugs dotted about on the floor. In between the rugs there were crayons lying about on the floor. Five little water colour and poster paint paint boxes, paint brushes, bits of charcoal, feathers, beads, coloured tissue paper, glue pots and jars of coloured water. There were little paintings and sketches lying about on the floor as well. On the walls of the room there were similar paintings and sketches, but all of these were mounted and framed behind glass in different sized wooden frames.

I wanted to look more closely at these sketches and paintings, so that was what I did. I entered the room fully and looked, moving from one to the next to the next and the next. All the paintings that I could see were children's paintings. Paintings of brightly coloured animals. Rivers and hills. Children playing. Children eating. Elephants flying towards the moon. Houses, and adults and children leaning out of the windows, laughing, and throwing a blue ball to a red dog. Throwing a blue ball into the rock garden in the middle of next doors pond. And paintings of flowers that bees had settled on with big grins across their faces. And the world with a big rocket heading towards it and not away from it. And a painting of vegetables grouped together on a table. There were vegetables and a painted cardboard sign propped up on the painted table that read, 'Please feel free to take any of these if you can use them'.

I left the room as I found it, pulling the door to as it had been before I entered the room. I walked a little further down the hall and there was a note pressed into a pin board on the hall wall. The note read, 'we've gone to the sea for sandwiches and pick-nick'. Back soon.

I took the words on the note as a licence then to roam freely about the house, since there obviously wasn't anybody there. The other partially opened doors off of the hallway were not as inviting as the stairs. That was what I heard myself thinking. I walked past the other three doorways not even bothering to look casually into any of the rooms behind them. I headed for the stairwell down by the door to the kitchen. I climbed the stairs.

At the top of the steep staircase there was an open door leading into a bedroom that was directly above the kitchen at the back of the house. The curtains in the room were drawn, but not fully, and there was a desk light on in the far corner of the room on a desktop. Above the desk was a wide cane blind that was unrolled crookedly to about three quarters of its full length. But the blind wasn't sheltering light from any window. I could see beneath the blind the outline of the bottom six inches or so of a wide cork pin board. There were photographs and bits of newspaper clipping poking out on the board from beneath the crooked bottom edge of the blind where it hadn't been unrolled fully.

To reach the desk, I had to move to the window and pass the curtains with the gap separating them, because the desk was tucked into a corner behind a large wooden double bed that ran along in front of the window, leaving a narrow corridor that led up to the desk.

Through the gap in the heavy dark curtains, I didn't expect to see anything much other than more wild garden, but what I actually saw was a deck chair at the far end of a beautifully mown lawn with Vera sitting in it reading a book. She obviously hadn't gone to the sea. The note downstairs must have been written for another day and simply left up on the hall pin board. Shit, what do I do now? That was what I was thinking.

I watched. Vera was in her back garden reading a book. I could see her. I could see a little group of children as well. Laughing. Playing ball. Skipping. Making up a play. Swapping hats and robes and shiny buckled shoes as the play moved from one scene to the next, unfolding out there on the lawn.

Vera read, and every so often, she'd rest the book in her lap. To watch the children playing. To help them tie a scarf or roll up the long trouser legs on a Prince or a King. To secure a necklace for a Princess or a Queen. To paint a new character face on one of her children. I saw her laughing. Making suggestions every so often from her deck chair about what might happen next when the children couldn't agree on the next part of whatever adventure it was that they were playing out.

I didn't feel awkward about watching all this, I don't know why, even though I was doing it from an upstairs bedroom inside of Vera's house. The fact that I was trespassing seemed irrelevant. I didn't feel frightened of being discovered. In fact, there was a part of me that wanted to be discovered.

I pulled away from the gap in the curtains and then I sat down on the edge of the bed to collect my thoughts. I moved along the edge of the bed to the desk to get a closer look at the photographs and newspaper clippings poking out on the pin board beneath the cane blind. Now that I was closer, through the gaps in the blind, I could see other thin veins of newsprint and little horizontal strips of different pictures. I reached out and pulled down on the cord at the side of the blind, so that the blind moved up over the pin board that was behind it.

In the middle of the pin board there was a newspaper photograph of a woman. The woman looked similar to Vera. Their hair styles were very different, but there was a strong resemblance between their facial features. This newspaper clipping was coloured with age, as were all the clippings on the board. There were dates on all of them, all within the year 1966. There were other smaller newspaper photographs of the same woman dotted about on the pin board. They were obviously all taken from the same original photograph.

And then there were headlines, '**Village in Shock. Young Single Mother Raped and Murdered as Six-Year-Old Daughter Is Made To Watch From Pushchair. Naked Raped and Murdered Mother Found in Village Copse. Rapist And Murderer of Young Mother Still At Large**'.

There were other actual photographs on the pin board. Full length pictures of Vera's mother in a thin cotton pastel coloured dress and black canvas slip on pumps, a little girl of five or six standing at her side. This little girl was the little girl that Vera used to be. She was wearing black canvas pumps the same as her mothers. She was smiling at the camera.

There were two or three other newspaper pictures pinned up in which neither Vera as a child or her mother appeared. These pictures were of my house. Not as it is now. The surroundings were very different. There was no driveway. Just a tangled and overgrown front garden. There was no road out front or house opposite. Just a narrow-unmade earth path where the road is now. There was a copse of dense high ferns that began where the limit of the overgrown front garden ended, and an open field with a single cow grazing in it where the house opposite now is.

I realised that for the last six months I had been watching Vera assume the final position of her mother's rape and murder at the spot where this actually took place thirty years previously. It was now a grass verge next to a road, but this wasn't how the little girl that Vera was saw it at all. It was still that spot in a dense fern copse where her mother's life brutally ended. An event which a five- or six-year-old Vera was forced to watch from her pushchair.

She didn't want to forget because she couldn't forget. Her mother's killer was long gone perhaps, but there was always a chance that someone might have seen, might actually have seen her, when they see me like you do, and remember everything about it.

I turned away from the pin board to find Vera standing in the bedroom doorway watching me. She had one of the canvas child's pumps in her hand. Thank you for returning this, she said. Now that you know everything would you please leave. Please. She stepped into the bedroom, leaving the doorway free for me to pass through.

I left the house. I walked home.

In the days that followed, Vera appeared again outside my house to lie naked on the verge as before. I noticed her, in the midst of my doing other things around the house. But I no longer watched her. And I no longer watch her now because:

Well, because I know what she's doing, and I know why she's doing it, that's all.

A Child On Mars

He loses a child - over the telephone.

From somewhere very far away across the land and across the sea, she lifts a receiver and dials. He lifts a receiver and answers. A very few words leak, via a tangle of cable, amidst tears and their shared gulps for air. It's all so very simple.

It's a fact of nature. Losing a child.

A fact that is so very simple to say.

Just four words.

Our child is lost.

And then:

He has to sit with himself, without her, a thousand miles from where it is that this thing has happened. He cannot touch her. He cannot see her. He can only wonder. He can only sit and wonder. She cannot touch him. She cannot see him. She can only sit and wonder.

He sits in his hollow foreign place thinking. Thinking, and then later drinking himself towards the sleep of reason. At least, this is what he hopes that booze and sleep will eventually give him. A reason.

There are people in the hotel room in which he sits that know him.

People standing and sitting just inches from him, as those four words and those other sounds from the woman that he loves beyond measure leak into his ears. These people though are not the people that he would choose to be with at this moment. They're colleagues of his, people with the sympathy skills of mice. This is not a moment for people like these. Their faces will not, he thinks, help him face the truth.

Amongst others, there is a woman there with him, a colleague woman there in that thousand-mile ruined hideaway country who believes herself to be in the reaches of pregnancy. This, for him, seems strangely perverse and inappropriate. Why her there at that moment of all moments? You see, this particular colleague woman wants to wish her own child away, wants to wipe it from inside her. Its father ran away in the night, a night of some time ago, taking an anxious face out under the stars.

The not wanting to be pregnant woman attempts to speak, forcing herself out amongst the awkward air that the expression of his face at the telephone has activated within the room. The woman attempts to offer words and something of herself to him, and to his curdled mess, lost on a patterned sheet a thousand miles from here. But perhaps better that she simply stands at the hotel room window watching the lake and the men there below plucking the small-scale fish out of its regions. Her eyes move to the window, to the bright sun outside, and to the fishermen below, when her words run out of steam at regular intervals. Language within the room, for this man and his newly lost child, hangs with its mouth open gulping for air.

There is suddenly a kind of silence there in the room, a silence that cannot be described. Time passes with such detail in those strange moments after this first telephone call with the woman has ended. He just sits and he looks. Looks at everything, at everybody, but at nothing in particular.

Then he looks at the telephone on the telephone table. He looks away. He looks at the telephone on the telephone table. He looks away. He rips the telephone from its moorings in the wall and throws it through the plate glass window thirty storeys from the ground. He throws the telephone out towards the sun. He leaves the hotel room, carrying his lost child inside his head. He leaves the smell of his instant grief hanging in the room for his pale faced colleagues to sniff at. He moves to the room next door. He picks up another telephone receiver and dials. Across the thousand miles of land and sea, she picks up her receiver and this time it is her that answers him. The news of his lost child is exactly as it was a few moments ago when he picked up the receiver in the room next door. Nothing has changed.

What are the pictures of his woman of a thousand miles away? What of her trial on the patterned sheets in the middle of the night, whilst staying with her closest girlfriend? How does her body feel? What does she actually say? How does she punctuate with words the feelings of her exhausted and empty shell? How does she even begin to speak to this 'father' who will now have to wait for that very pleasure within another span of months? She cannot say what the words are to help them both. She and he and all of the rest of everyone with their relative cancers, road accidents and old age dying moments must all struggle without the aid of a good strong net.

Over the telephone, a thousand miles apart, with their lost child circling inside their heads, they bluster together like a pair of languageless infants. The telephone story that she tells doesn't have many words, but mostly just sounds. No good words worthy of literary prizes, just plenty of sounds that might interest a passing saucer of aliens. And then suddenly, in the midst of her telephone story the phone does what their child had been forced to do in the middle of the night before. It goes dead. Her story is not even a paragraph to write home about when somebody somewhere, or something somewhere disconnects the telephone connection. He is left hanging there without her. She is left hanging there without him.

The problem is a technical hitch, which later becomes a technical nightmare. Somewhere in the thousand-mile tangle of cable that separates them, it has been decided that they may not speak again until hours have passed.

They are left to their own devices. To imagine what they must imagine, alone and separate. To picture each other as each may or may not be.

They cannot make any sense, alone and separate, of their child that has left the world. It will never make sense. Not in a week, or a month, or months or a year. He thinks about the great many things that mother earth does have time for, those which it organises with such detail and courtesy, and then he thinks about particular deaths and particular griefs and how these seem to be left to wander on their own to find a time for themselves.

He opens the flaking hotel window up in the sky and rages to the innocent fishermen below. They swear back at him in a language that he doesn't know head nor tail of but knows that they wouldn't use that same language in front of their children.

He wishes he could fly, or better still vaporise and materialise at will. He asks God for something, but since his speakings together with God have never been on a regular basis, he knows full well that God will have no choice but to put him on hold whilst it's dishing out the prizes elsewhere for that day.

And then, all that he can think about is the getting home principal.

He drove a thousand miles to where he is. He knows that he must drive a thousand miles to where it is that he must be.

The getting home principal is a number of different things, at different times, for the purpose of achieving one and the same goal. That of getting home, principally. It is the ability given to a person to squash time and to eat up continental road systems with utter recklessness without recourse to personal, or collective safety. It is a state of being that allows a person to feel totally comfortable about being rude, angry and uncivilised to any and all other persons that are encountered in places like cafes, petrol filling stations and at customs control.

He drives. He eats. He smokes. He cries. He doesn't sleep when he breaks his journey to lay his head down in a Belgian roadside motel.

And what is his woman thinking. His woman whose body has flushed away a life in the night. She knows nothing of the man and the different tortured faces that he carried with him when those first four words of hers leaked into his ears. She knows nothing of how those other strange alien sounds from her were acting inside his head. She knows nothing of the not wanting to be pregnant woman colleague, or of the awkward air that reigned in that thousand mile away hotel room filled with those other pale faces. All she knows is of her own sudden fear, a fear and feeling that woke her to her senses in the darkness of a night. All she knows is of the trial that then unfolded from inside her. Her child, their child, suddenly seeing the artificial light from a 60-watt bulb through unformed eyes on an unformed face, face down on a patterned sheet in a swamp of thick electric liquid shot from her body. All she knows is of her closest girlfriend who witnessed the trial, a witness bleary eyed and disturbed suddenly by strange screams in the night.

There were no shared notes of the trial on record for either the mother or the father to refer to when they finally stood together again in the same time at the same place to give evidence to one another. He smelt of tobacco and sweat and lack of sleep. She stood very still, wearing a patterned dress, but he knew that she was naked beneath it, because this was how it always was.

They stood together in the sun, the same sun that had burned them both in the days before, though they had been separated by a thousand miles of land and sea. They stood together in the sun, at the garden gate to their house. They touched like they always did, and he could suddenly hear inside his head the strange telephone language that had passed between them that last time that they had spoken.

They went inside their house. They locked the doors. And time went by.

They tried to speak, to convince one another of their individual styles of grief during the time that they had been apart. They wanted to hear each other's stories. They asked for precise details of what each of them had done, in the hope that somehow these details might connect and help them both to make sense of what had happened. They wanted to make the experience of their lost child an experience that did not separate them. An experience that they were not separated by.

He held in his head imagined graphic pictures of his child bleeding its way into the light, amidst violent screaming that the child itself couldn't hear, but no matter how hard he tried, he couldn't conjure in his head the different postures of the woman's body whilst this was happening. He couldn't see any of the gestures that she was making or where on her body the tears that she had shed were falling. He could not imagine it happening where it was that she had told him that it had happened.

For him it had happened in a placeless place that could only ever be inside his head. The event of his lost child was literally lost in space inside his head. He had nothing at all to anchor it to, even though he knew for a fact that it had actually happened somewhere.

All of the things that he needed to pin his child's death down were locked between the woman herself and her closest friend, this sole expert witness.

Some weeks after his return, he arranged to see the closest friend, in order he hoped to steal from her the experience of hers that should have been his. He wanted to know precisely what her language and gestures had been as his baby had begun its journey to Mars or wherever it was that the baby was heading that was not of the same world that was his.

They sat together in an orchard, the man and the closest friend, and the man tried desperately to steal the things that should have been his. He should have been arrested because it was an impossible job and one that he should never have taken on. He didn't have the right tools for the job simply because the right tools had still to be invented. He couldn't rip that time shared between the two women from its moorings and make it his. All he wanted of course was something that was real.

But he had to let the closest friend have what was hers. He had to let the woman whom he loved beyond measure have what was hers. He had to let his lost child be lost in space somewhere lost inside his head. He had no choice about any of these things.

And when all is said and all is done, the man wishes his woman to know that in the walls of a particular hotel room a thousand miles far distant, there are the fossil markings of him on the telephone to her, as she tells him that their child is lost.

There are the markings of this same man's desperate tears. There are the markings of this same man who doesn't know which way to turn. The markings of a helpless man feeding his tears to strangers. The markings of a man who wanted there and then to invent a time machine to turn things backward. The markings of a man who wanted to invent a language that would bridge how the death of a child might be shared at a distance. The markings of that man in that room a thousand miles away in the sky will always be there as a witness to his grief.

And again, when all is said and all is done, the man hopes that if it ever became possible for him to travel to Mars, well, he hopes that the woman would understand and ask no questions if she were to see him packing his bags to leave one day and catch the next available flight.

Something To Remember Me By

Words from a woman who believes herself to be of no importance:

'There are coins, a small hill of salt and an egg. A cork, a penknife, and a pair of spectacles. There's a marble, a shell, and a clothes peg. A paper clip and a cocktail stick. There's a cheap silver ring of no consequence and a porcelain teacup. There are scissors and an HB pencil with a perfectly sharpened point. And there's a pink bus ticket for a journey that I made five years ago to attend my father's funeral.

I am an artist. For days on end, I arrange and then re-arrange these things on a circular mahogany tray. Each arrangement is carefully photographed a number of times before moving on to a different arrangement. I like to make small objects from the world sit together in configurations that they would never, in the normal course of events, find themselves.

What is the true relationship between coins and spectacles, between salt and a paper clip? How should things be? How should things not be?

I make other pieces of work in which, for example, I allow apples of different varieties to die. To rot away in their own fashion nestled in glass lead sealed boxes. In one glass box an apple sits alone. In another the apple is surrounded by sugar, or cotton wool, or wood or earth or salt or newspaper. These boxes rest on a low wooden table adjacent to a bed. A bed that rests on a fake wooden slatted floor. The white linen duvet of the bed has a corner carefully turned back to reveal turfs of grass where the white linen sheets would otherwise be. Littered across the turf are wind fall apples resting on the damp grass. Hidden beneath one of the linen pillows at the head of the bed there is a small tape recorder. It plays the tape of a woman's voice. My voice. I say, over and over again, 'Will it always be like this. Will it always be like this'.

Adjacent to the bed, but opposite to the low table, there is a small wooden window frame suspended in the air at chest height. One of the panes of glass in this window frame has been purposefully smashed. On the low table, amongst the ranks of glass apple boxes, there is a notebook containing handwritten mathematical equations. Calculations to establish who knows what? At the base of the bed, resting on the false slatted wooden floor, there is a large clear glass water pitcher that contains still black motor sump oil. Next to the pitcher there is an empty crystal glass. There is nobody present within this fake half- formed room, but it is clear that 'something' has happened there.

This was a piece of work that many would be proud of.

I make other pieces of work in which, for example:

I establish a bank of telephone and video phone lines between a room in London and a room in Belfast. I invite people from both locations simply to talk with one another. That's all. Just talk. It's very simple. Children talking to children. Children talking to adults. Adults talking to other adults. Out of the window from the particular room in London, it is possible to see clearly Big Ben and the Houses of Parliament - if you care to look that is.
There are many other pieces of work which will have to be left for another time.

You have a small sample, and this is sufficient for now.

You see, I'd like to tell you something of my father. He blew up buildings. For a living. Doing such things helped keep the wolf from the door as he would always say. He made a point of saying as well that the wolf was always hungry. I remember wondering as a child where it was that this wolf might live since, from what my father said, it must have been reasonably close by. I told him this one day and he simply beamed a broad smile at me.

K L xx'

As a child, I spent hours sitting in my father's study at home watching him plan his work. A daughter finding out what father does and exactly how he does it.

There were charts of some of the buildings that he had destroyed framed around the walls of the study. There were photographs of him, proud in his hard hat, at various sites around the world. Photographs of him on site before and after his meticulous acts of destruction.

My father saw his work as being very necessary in the wider scheme of things. He said that destroying buildings that had outlived their use reminded people of their own mortality, which he felt was a justification for what he did. People need a poke in the back of the head every so often he would say, to make them think about who they are, where they are and where they're going.

I am called an artist because I bring things into the world that would otherwise not be there. I arrange things that do exist, arrange them in strange situations. I make things that do not already exist because I, and I think other people, like the possibility of other possibilities in the world. I like to create things as they might be, to suggest that things could be different if only.......

But I know that I am only one person. However, I believe that this can make a difference. At least this was how I used to feel, but things are changing.

My father died in very funny circumstances that were also very tragic:

It had been raining. His shoes were very wet and slippery. He entered a building with a marble floored foyer, a building which contained a person who wished him to destroy another building. He was in a hurry. Late for his meeting. He slipped on the marble floor on approaching a marble staircase. He lost his balance and fell, his head striking a solid marble staircase banister embellishment. He fell with such force that his skull shattered, and I remember him dying in a nearby hospital a short while after this.

He and I were a one parent family. My mother left him years before for a one-armed band leader. She was in search of romance and champagne and concert tours in front of the rich who have such a taste for good things.

He died. I sold the house. I bought another house. I married a man who has two arms and a huge penis, and I did this to spite my mother.

My mother even now continues to write, pleading for forgiveness, but I burn all her letters. I keep the ashes in a special glass decanter on a south facing windowsill next to another special glass decanter that contains my father's ashes.

I like to think that by placing these two objects in such close proximity my father will understand the real love that I have for him. My father, in life, was a great admirer of irony.

Amongst the ashes in his decanter, I know that a small corner mouth smile lives on.

My husband has more than two good arms and a penis to envy.

He writes stories for children. Writes worlds for children to play in. Writes worlds for the children that we do not ourselves have. I used to love this man, but something has happened to me, and I no longer love anything that exists.

We talk so much together, but I could never tell him this.

I am called an artist because I bring things into the world. But over the years I have noticed that nothing changes. Things happen as they otherwise would in spite of everything that I do.

I am only one person and perhaps that is precisely the problem.

We now live in a huge house, my husband and I, and it's very near to the sea. The sea frightens me, but I cannot resist it.

As a child, before my mother left with the man whose Bach got the better of her, mother father and daughter lived together also by the sea.

In the winter this triangle of family would walk and search in rivers and caves and forests. In the summer we would spend long days together fiddling about on the beach.

Our favourite beach was at the bottom of a very sheer chalk cliff. Getting down to it from the cliff top was painstaking and arduous, but it was always worth it when we got there.

I liked to collect things as a child, and this beach, along with the rivers and caves and forests, was always full of strange childish treasures. I'd search about and put my findings into a little black canvas bag.

My mother would begin sunning herself as soon as we arrived at the beach, but my father would join in the finding fun with me. He had his own satchel for putting his things in. We collected and collected and collected.

After each visit to the beach, and when we arrived home, I'd empty out my bag and my father would empty out his satchel onto the big wooden kitchen table. My father and I would sort the different things out into their different groups. Then I'd gather up these groups, put them into separate boxes and hide them in my room.

There were all these different little worlds, worlds of feathers, leaves, shells, flat stones, stones with holes in, stones with crystals in, types of bark, fishing hooks, interesting bare sticks, shoes, flowers grouped together and pressed according to colour and size, dollies bits and pieces, plastic combs, plastic animals. All these different little worlds hidden in boxes beneath my bed.

These trips to that beach at the bottom of the chalk cliff seemed to go on for years and years and then, after one particular trip, we never went back again.

I described this particular trip to my husband who said that he wanted to write it out as a story. He said that he wanted to write it out in a language that I might have used at the age that I was when it happened. What follows is what he wrote, and this is how what happened, happened:

'It is a very plain day today for our day at the beach. At our beach at the bottom of the cliff. A plain day with a hard wind running across our faces. Father and mother and me.

I am called Morgan. Named after those very fancy cars that rich people have. I am nine years old and today is my birthday. My favourite present comes for me right at the end of this day. It is a peacock feather.

On this day I have my bag, my bag that smells of rivers and caves and forests and the sea and ruined buildings. I am searching for I don't know what until I find it. That's the best way to search because otherwise you only ever find what you want to find, and sometimes not even that which means that you end up going home disappointed.

On this day, my mother does not do the sunning of herself as usual. The wind that's here today together with the sun will peel her skin she says all greatly fed up. And so, dragging her heels, she searches with my father.

He says that four eyes is better than two, but I don't agree which is why I'm doing it with just my two on my own. There's a book full of real things here to look up the name for when we get home.

Today, everything that seems to be here is supposed to be here, which probably means that people haven't been here, or else their unreal things have been washed on the midnight tide to another place along the way of other beaches elsewhere. People do leave things and lose things out of their mouths and out of their pockets, but these are not people like me or my father, though I cannot speak truthfully of my mother in the self-same way.

She is one of those laws unto herself.

So, we are on this beach and our six eyes are working as hard as diamonds. Their four together and my two trying to uncover some of the things of interest. On and under rocks and stones. At the shoreline. At the base of the difficult cliff. Noticing things out of the corners of our six eyes and sometimes honing in on them for a closer look and sometimes not.

We each start to pick things up after a time. I put my things in my bag, down into its confusing smelly old depths. My mother and father do the same with my father's satchel which smells of tobacco and brand after brand of suntan oil.

We never share our finds where it is that we are. That always and only ever happens on the big wooden table in the kitchen when we get home at the end of the day and have got ourselves all normal again.

That's when we share all our finds.

On the big wooden table which is nothing at all like the place that the real things that we find were first in. This means that we can see them more clearly for what they in themselves are, because there's not the rest of their nature around about to crowd in on them.

I have one or two things in the darkness of my bag, and they have either none, or one, or just a few things in the tobacco and sun oil darkness of the satchel, and that's when I hear my father shout my name.

I look up and towards him and see him pointing into the sky. His face is an unusual shape. He has never used this shape before when he has used my name. It isn't a shape for me or this beach.

I look up into the sky to where it is that his finger is pointing.

There is a motor car that is on fire, and it is in the sky, gliding out over the edge of the cliff top. I cannot hear the sound that it is making, because from way down where I am, the sea against the shoreline mixed in with the wind is making such a massive noise.

I watch this motor car glide all on fire in the sky, as it makes its big curve in the air back towards the earth and down towards the sea. A ball of red flame in the blue sky that isn't the sun.

I don't know what to do, so I don't do anything. I just stand there where I am, with a face shape like my fathers on my face.

My father does know what to do it seems, because, as the motor car hits the surface of the sea, he is right there diving into the sea and already swimming towards the motor car which is even now filling up with water very fast.

There are people in the motor car. Two people. A man and a woman, and I am running down the beach now towards the sea because I want to know what will happen to them.

My mother is shouting to my father that its useless to do what he's doing, but since she isn't doing anything to help, I think she should just stay where she is and wait in silence until we know what is real here.

The car has gone now.
Underneath the water.
And so has my father.

But I know that that isn't it, because my father is such a big man and a very good swimmer indeed. He might be shot or run over by a car or train someday, but he couldn't drown because that wouldn't be right.

For a while there is just the sea there and my mother and me standing on the beach looking for signs of life. One comes and it is two heads above the water. My father and another man. Then, shortly after this, there is a third head. It is a woman's head.

Then my father starts shouting at my mother and my mother runs into the sea, careful to take off her lovely beach clothes before she does this. She swims to where they all are and then my mother and father shout some more at one another, before they start to swim back to the shore, each dragging one of the motor car people with them. I still don't know what to do, so, like before, I don't do anything except stand there, watching and wondering what will happen next.

Then there are four people on the shore, just in front of the water's edge. Two of them lying flat on their stomachs, the man, and the woman from the motor car. My mother and father are sitting astride one each of them, pushing down on their backs very hard, as if they're on two fairground horses that have unexpectedly stopped mid-ride, and my mother and father are trying to gee them up to move again.

My father shouts at me not to look on at all this that's going on, but instead to continue looking at things of interest from nature until they've managed to sort everything out.

Since I am more interested in the two people on their stomachs being pumped away at, I make out as if I haven't heard my father because of the loud sound that the sea is making, and since my father is so busy with them himself, he doesn't notice that I don't go off a searching as he has asked.

During the time that the pumping is happening, my mother and father make many faces that I have never seen them make before. They pump for a long time but neither the man nor the woman move at all. Well, not a bit of them like they're alive anyway.

Eventually, my mother and father stop what they're doing and stand up on the beach together.

My father begins to cry and then so does my mother, but I don't believe her. They move together to hug one another, standing like this looking down at the two people who are very still, lying not far from the sea on the shoreline, just as if they've been washed up like porpoises and seals are sometimes.

I walk down the beach to where my mother and father are standing, and I stand with them looking down.

My father gathers my head in his wet hands and presses my face into his wet clothes. He's hoping that I will not see the two dead people at as close a range as this because it would upset me. I know that they are dead and can therefore use this word, because they are as still on the beach there as some of the pets that I have had which died in the night and are very still in the morning.

The corner of one of my eyes isn't hidden in my father's wet clothes. Its right there looking at the dead people. They have parts of their bodies that have been burned from the motor car fire. There are clothes and parts of their bodies that have twisted together so you can't tell one from the other. They both have funny faces on them, faces that you never see in the street.

I am looking at the woman's face, at the side of the woman's face, with its other side pressing down hard into the stones of the beach. Looking at the woman's ear and the earring in that same ear, which has part of a peacock feather hanging from it. The feather is all wet and spread out along the line of the woman's jawbone. I know the feathers from a peacock because I've seen them before. This would be a thing of interest from nature if I'd seen it where it should be, like near to where a peacock is or might be, but of course there aren't any peacocks here because this isn't where they live. I couldn't therefore take it as a thing of interest from nature, but I could take it if I thought of it as a birthday present.

We gather up our things. My father says we must go now. Climb the difficult cliff, and when we get to the top, head for a phone box and phone people that can take care of all this. It somehow seems very odd to just leave the two people there where they are pressing down into the stones. To just walk away with them there not shivering even though they would be if they were alive.

Whilst the gathering up is happening and the backs of my mother and father are turned, I bend down on the beach just by the woman's face. I reach out with my hand and quickly remove the peacock earring from her ear. Then I put it carefully in my canvas bag.

We never search anywhere again after this. And I suppose that this is because we are perhaps frightened of finding things that might be just too real for our own good. The end.'

My husband finished his story at this point, but the real story continued. The rest of it happened for me years after I was nine, which was why my husband stopped where he did.

My father obviously followed the developing story of these two people in the car as this was revealed in the newspapers over the weeks and months that elapsed after their death at our beach.

I know this because when my father died, and I was clearing out his study prior to selling his house, I came across a file of newspaper cuttings that he had collected and kept, that related to these people. I took these cuttings and many other things with me, including certain bits and pieces from the heavy metal shed that my father also worked in that was hidden away at the bottom of our very long and large garden. As a child I was forbidden to enter this shed, especially when my father was in there working. This metal shed is a story which my husband will never write about on my behalf because, you see, I have kept it to myself.

But what of those two dead people on the beach? What was their story?

They had a house. They had two young children. They had a happy life and then.....

The man set the house on fire, and he did this on purpose. Then the man put the barrel of a gun to the head of one of his children. He pulled the trigger. He put the barrel of the same gun to the head of his other child. Again, he pulled the trigger. He forced his wife at gunpoint to carry each child in turn out to the garage at the side of their remote house and to lay them in the boot of the family car. He forced his wife to shut the boot of the car with her dead children inside. He put the barrel of the gun to the head of his wife, the mother of these children, and forced her to sit in their car with him whilst he drove it at a reasonable speed towards the coast and towards the edge of the one-hundred-and-fifty-foot chalk cliff.

Fifty-two feet and six inches from the edge of the cliff itself, he slammed his foot down hard on the car's accelerator. And at some point, during these last fifty-two feet of earth there was an electrical breakdown in the vehicles wiring system, which accounted for the flames that I saw escaping from the car as it flew out into the sky above me.

The electrical breakdown part of the story was included in the cuttings that I read presumably as a way of highlighting how clever the police now are in detecting the side order issues within their detective enquiries.

This man murdered his children, staged an accident in which he knew that himself and his wife would also die, because he couldn't bear the thought of facing the truth. And the truth was that he was a greedy fucker.

A greedy fucker, who gambled heavily. The gambling began small scale, but with his greed it grew bigger and bigger, to the point where he had gambled away the family house and everything in it.

He killed his family and himself because his nasty little habit overran him completely to the point where he couldn't face himself or anyone else. He wanted everything but ended his life in total shame.

I look at myself. I look at my own greed for things which has not as yet reached a shameful degree.

I am an artist who arranges objects in the world to discover what their relationships might be. To reveal for myself and other people something about the real things that surround us.

The things that I bring into the world are simple things. Things that people have forgotten how to see, or rather no longer wish to see, because they'd rather see the things from Sony or Zanussi or IBM, or any of the like of them.

I am only one person. One person who at one time believed that she might make a difference. That she might make people see. But I now see myself that Sony or Zanussi or IBM move much faster than I could ever move. That they see much more clearly than I have ever seen.

What is the relationship between a person and the things in which they believe? Is it still possible for one person to change things? Who is kidding who these days?

I no longer wish to call myself anything, least of all an artist, but I do have a plan, and with this plan my father will help me.

Words from the husband of a woman who believes herself to be of no importance:

My wife Morgan used to be an artist, but she doesn't do that anymore. She gave it all up.

She burnt all of the beautiful things that she made, which used to decorate our house. I came home one day to find her in the garden, in the process of destroying her work. Smashing things to pieces with a hammer, burning what could be burnt. And now there is nothing of her anywhere.

She cleared out her studio at the bottom of our garden. She whitewashed all its windows. She padlocked its door in three places. She nailed its door sealed into the door frame.

Much time goes by in which she does nothing. In which she is afraid to leave the house.

And then there is much time in which she does nothing other than read newspapers. She insists that these newspapers must not be destroyed. They lie in high piles in various rooms of the house that we share together.

And then one day, and for many other once weekly days I find her:

She's in the attic.

Propping up her chin in the attic with a gloved hand. A thin fingered industrial glove. Thin fingered for delicate acts. For delicate work. A beautiful chin cupped in a rough but delicate glove. Her two toughened elbows melded, almost, but not quite, into the cold steel of the tabletop. A metal table with her standing behind it in front of a metal chair. This is the position in which she always begins her acts in the attic. I've seen her.

In the beginning, her two slate grey eyes nailing thoughts to the orange wall in front of her. An orange room you see - attic orange. Don't ask me why. Ask her. And if she tells you, keep it to yourself because I don't want to know why. That's a lie, of course.

She's lit up there, mostly, but not exclusively, by a bold angle-poise on the cold old table. Other sources of light and heat, I'll come to later, but as I say, mostly its Mr angle-poise. Off and on. On and off. Now you see me, now you don't. Stretches of one or the other, sometimes for fifteen minutes or more. Other times it's off and on off and on off and on, the muscles in her index finger on overtime.

I've seen her. Her messages of darkness and light pitching their way moonward through the attic skylight, but who the hell to?

Ah, now you know how nosy parker knows - '**Husband Spying On Wife Through Attic Skylight Is Never Caught In The Act**'.

All's quiet in the attic room, but I know she's up there. Because the day is Sunday. And that's her day for nailing thoughts to orange walls. The day for sharpening her mind through dangerous acts. Other days of the week are for other things, like me and the rest of the world, but Sunday is for the game of thinking clear and useful thoughts with the real possibility always in mind that a hand might be lost, or part of an arm, or the side of a face that I love.

Industrial gloves you see. That's the key. Albeit thin fingered industrial gloves, but industrial gloves, nevertheless.

You see, on Sundays, thinking that I know nothing of it, she takes fireworks apart. To sharpen her mind, to end the week on a high note, to possibly lose the side of her face. It isn't funny.

November the 5th every Sunday. I worry about not warning the cats and dogs of neighbours, but how could I put it to them, without seeming ridiculous. They'd want a ream of reasons wouldn't they, that I wouldn't be able to provide. I say nothing of course because what could I say?

I remember the children's chant, '**Light Up The Sky With Standard Fireworks**'. The advert chant from years ago.

When Sunday comes, something like this chant comes by to haunt me. The words are different though. They've become warped with thought and real concern. '**Look At That Woman With One Arm, With One Arm, With One Arm, And How Does She Cope With The Children - Assuming That She Has Any?**'

She doesn't appear to be worried by anything that Standard might throw at her. Rockets, Roman Candles, Catherine Wheels, and Bangers. They're all the same to her. Some, of course, might be more difficult to prise apart than others, but she has the tools for each and every idiosyncrasy that they might have.

She has blades and clips and pins. Scissors, chunky, fine, thin, long, short, and forceful. And. Wait for it. She has these plastic goggles as well. Now they should be serious goggles, but they're not. Serious I mean for the task at hand, i.e., trying to avoid losing your face. But they're not. They're the same goggles that she uses when she swims. Ridiculous. She looks ridiculous with these attempts at personal safety on. I know this because I've seen her. '**Nosy Parker Reveals Himself**'.

Months ago, she started going up to the attic room, refusing to tell me what she was doing. 'I just need regular time to think alone', she said. Okay. That was fine. Of course, it was. No problem with that. Who me? Certainly not.

Maybe a month went by, and I began to wonder. To wonder how precisely it was that she thought up in the attic every Sunday. I wasn't interested necessarily in what it was that she thought, but more how it was that she did this.

The attic.

It wasn't a room that I'd ever used. In fact, since we'd moved into the house, the attic was the one room that had remained neglected. There was nothing in it - just bare floorboards and a small open fireplace. At least that's what I thought, from the last time that I'd ventured up there before she'd started using it of a Sunday.

Sundays went by and by as they do. She was up there having her time to think.

And that's what I began to do. To think. To think about what it is that I need in order to be able to think usefully for periods of time.

I thought of comfort. I can't think unless I'm comfortable. That's important. Yes, it is. Very. I'd need at least a chair in a room to even begin to think about spending time thinking. And a comfortable chair at that. Somewhere and something to lie down on would also be really helpful. Now she had nothing though, barely nothing, not even a comfy chair. She never took cushions up there with her or anything like that.

I got really curious, as I say, about how she was doing what she said she wanted to do with no aids of any kind at all. Did she stand in a corner? Lie on the rough floorboards and stare at the ceiling? Or squat huddled in a corner for safety? My thoughts went round and round about how she thought her thoughts.

The attic has a skylight with a wrought iron ladder leading to it that runs down the side of the house. Down the side of all five storeys of my home for evacuation purposes in the event of a fire.

Ha bloody ha! It isn't funny.

She always used the interior stairs.

She didn't like rain, and open heights were not good to her.

After six or seven months of her Sunday thoughts, I couldn't resist it. I climbed the iron ladder and when I reached the top, I pressed my face against the skylight to see what she was up to. I thought at first that I was looking through somebody else's skylight.

There was a woman down there standing behind a six-foot square metal table with a white lab assistants coat on and swimming goggles. A mass of unruly hair gathered in clumps on the back of her head with an assortment of elastic bands.

The walls of the room were orange, and there was a roaring fire in the grate. It was Morgan. This woman down there below. It was Morgan my wife, in our fucking now orange attic, cutting open fireworks.

There were boxes of fireworks piled high in one corner of the room, and then on the top of this metal table, little mounds of gun powder, rocket sticks, empty firework casings and fuse lengths, all gathered separately but with great precision.

Where had all this gear come from? What the hell did she think she was doing, and where the fuck was the bucket of water, the bucket of sand, or the fire extinguisher just in case?

I remember looking at the fire roaring in the grate and then my eyes darting through the skylight around the attic room, searching for her safety precautions. But there weren't any. Not a jot of safety anywhere.

I also remember thinking over and over again - this is my wife Morgan, a woman that I thought I knew. Knew a lot about. Knew most about. Yes, it is her, isn't it? Christ it is. How could I not know? How could she not tell me that on a regular basis she dismantles fireworks in our attic room with only a pair of swimming goggles to protect her face from possible meltdown. Jesus, what the hell had happened between us to bring things to this?

I thought of banging on the skylight window there and then. Then thought better of it, because probably this would startle her, and God knows the consequences of startling a woman when she's carefully dismantling fireworks in your attic.

I didn't do this. My mouth went all dry. My head was racing with all the possible what to dos. What did I do? I climbed back down the iron ladder. I let myself back into the house. I went up to the bedroom that Morgan and I shared.

I sat in a chair in the bedroom. I stood in a corner in the bedroom. I laid down on the bed in the bedroom, thinking all the while. Thinking about what I was going to say. What it was that the two of us might talk about from here on into the future. When I was thinking, I kept noticing how much listening my ears were doing. They were picking up no end of things. Clocks, water cisterns, the wind outside, trains. But nothing at all of Morgan's movements in the attic.

After about an hour she appeared at the bedroom door. No white coat, no goggles, no gloves. All of her face, and all of her limbs still where they should be. 'Hi', she said. 'Thank you', she said. She came and sat on the bed, reached out a hand and touched me on the face. 'I love you', she said. Then she said, 'what are you thinking about', and I said the first thing that came into my head, because I was still all of a dither between my ears. And I said, 'oranges' funnily enough. 'I just fancy an orange.', I said.

I made a point of emphasising the word orange but, there wasn't even a flicker in her eyes. 'I'll get you one', she said, and off she went. She came back a couple of minutes later with two oranges. She laid down on the bed next to me and nothing more, I couldn't get any words into my mouth about fireworks and her up there in the attic. I didn't know how to start the attic thing off.

We slept.

The next day I followed her. When she left the house, I followed her, hoping that she might do something, go somewhere, meet someone that might give me some clues.

It felt really awkward. Following my wife. Tailing her like some flat nosed Private Dick. Dick Detective without any of the proper gear. It's embarrassing. But it isn't funny. Following someone. Someone that you know intimately. Can you imagine it?

Morgan started her day by walking from our house to the park nearby. She didn't speak to anyone because there was nobody else there but her. She was there for an hour. Sitting on a bench and looking at trees. At birds. At the sky. And at some photographs that she took out of her shoulder bag.

I had binoculars. Binoculars that had at one time belonged to her father. I could see that what she was looking at were photographs, but I couldn't see what these photographs were photographs of. She wasn't flicking through them like they were holiday snaps. Things were much more considered than they would be in holiday snap mentality. She got through only half a dozen in the hour that she was there. Between the sky and the birds and a cigarette or two.

When the hour was up, she put the photographs back in her bag, and returned to the house, knowing that I wouldn't be there because under normal circumstances I wouldn't be. I'd be out of the house until late working in my writing studio in town. Writing out fantastic worlds for children to play in.

This is how Morgan describes what I do to anybody that needs to know. But today I'm not. Today I'm snooping around trying not to look stupid, spying on my wife. Watching my own house and its contents, particularly my wife, for clues about something.

Fifty minutes in the house she was. Appearing and then disappearing at different windows. Christ, that was a long fifty minutes. Longest that I can remember. Ever.

I tried all sorts of vantage points to see what she might be up to, but nothing. No clues. Just various sightings of her passing windows. Watering pot plants around the house.

A big nothing to report.

Then there were no sightings of her. For three hours. And then I saw the skylight in the attic being pushed open.

I walked back to the house, but I didn't go inside. I climbed the wrought iron ladder at the side of the house until I reached the attic skylight. I peered down through the space that was available now that this was open, trying to be as quiet as possible.

The attic room had changed again.

Things had been cleared away, though where they had been cleared away to, I had no idea. There were no longer bits and pieces of fireworks everywhere. The metal tabletop had been cleared completely, apart from an old black canvas bag that Morgan had had for years, which was sitting on the tabletop.

Morgan was standing over it, buckling the bag shut, so I couldn't see what it was that the bag contained. Morgan had her heavy outdoor coat on. She picked the bag up and slung its shoulder strap over her shoulder. Then she turned towards the attic door and disappeared from view.

A short while after this, I heard the heavy front door of the house slam shut. I climbed down the wrought iron ladder, to see Morgan walking off up the road.

I followed her.

She walked to the station. She brought a cheap day return to London to include Underground travel. The woman at the ticket desk told me this and so I brought a similar ticket.

I was still working very hard at not being seen by Morgan. I even began to feel a little pleased with myself at how good I was getting at not being seen by her since I'd never done this kind of thing before.

Morgan got out of the train at Victoria. She left the station, and then she walked. It was getting on for 9pm by the time that we'd arrived in London.

I hate London, particularly during the January sales, and we were in London at precisely this time - at the height of the January sales. Even though it was nine o'clock in the evening, there were still thousands of people milling about.

Morgan walked and walked and walked.

She walked first to the Houses of Parliament.

She stood on Westminster bridge and gazed at this government building.

She walked from there to Buckingham Palace via Whitehall, Trafalgar Square and then down along The Mall.

She stood in front of Buckingham Palace for an hour. The Queen was at home but she didn't come out and say hello to Morgan, or to anyone else.

After an hour she left the Queen be, so that the Queen could carry on doing whatever it is that she does late on a Monday evening in January inside her ridiculous house.

Morgan walked, and she walked some more.

She walked around the heart of London from Monday night and intoTuesday morning.

And I walked with her.

Always at a careful and safe distance behind.

It never occurred to me to confront her.

It seemed that she was doing what she wanted to do, and that this was making her happy.

As the night went on, her walking pace didn't seem to tire at all.

She never once stopped to eat or drink anything.

She walked around the heart of London and stood at a distance from many of the buildings of power. Buildings inside which powerful things happened. Buildings from which powerful things came mostly very secretively out into the world.

She looked at all of these buildings, with such care and attention as if she was trying to discover what their secrets were. Not the foul secrets that were generated from inside of them, or even those that escaped to rip people's lives apart in the world outside.

She was looking for the secrets of the buildings in themselves, hoping to discover how they in themselves managed to encourage the greed that they housed.

At five o'clock in the morning she walked to Oxford Street.

She stood in front of shop window after shop window, seeing herself reflected in mirrors and glass amongst the many wonderful and necessary things that the various shops contained.

In a wide sensitively and neatly paved passageway, between two large well known stores, she sat down on a damp slatted wooden bench, behind which a thin sorry for itself tree had all but given up stretching out to the artificial light provided by the two stores to its left and right. The tree looked as if it didn't want to be there anymore, but of course it had no choice.

Morgan sat on the bench and looked at the bright orange and yellow paper bands that were placed in the store's windows at strategic places, advertising things like: '**40% REDUCTIONS ON OUR MOST EXPENSIVE ITEMS**'.

The one that I liked the most was this one:
'**SPEND THOUSANDS AND YOU WILL SAVE THOUSANDS. WE CAN'T SAY FAIRER THAN THAT CAN WE?**'

Morgan's father would have appreciated that one I'm certain.

It was now six o'clock in the morning.
Morgan suddenly looked dazed and tired; I suppose because she had finally sat down. Had finally stopped walking.
I was completely trashed, but I still wanted to know what the fuck she was up to.

It wasn't long after thinking this that I found out what she was up to.
She pulled the black canvas bag around her shoulder and placed it on her lap.
She opened the bag and took two things out from it.
The first thing was a portable tape recorder.
The second thing was a black leather handbag, a handbag that she only ever used on very special occasions. Occasions like funerals and our wedding for example.

She got up from the bench and walked towards a rubbish bin about twenty or thirty feet from the bench.

She dropped the tape recorder and the handbag into the bin.

She walked back to the bench and sat down again.

She pulled the black canvas bag around her shoulder and placed it on her lap once more.

She opened the canvas bag.

She took some wires out of it that I thought must be wires to her Walkman, but nothing went into her ears. Then, she waited.

She sat there waiting. Waiting for it to get light. Waiting for hungry shoppers to appear, which they did as they always do.

What the fuck was she up to?

There was light and then there were people. Lots of people. Milling about. I saw her take something out of the pocket of her coat. I saw her fiddling with the wires from her canvas bag. Fiddling with these and the thing that she had taken out of her coat pocket.

I saw her begin to sweat heavily, the beads of her nerves running down across her face, and then I suddenly realised what the fuck she was up to.

But my realising was all just a little bit too late in the day.

There was a switch on this thing that she had taken out of her coat pocket.

After shed connected this thing to the wires coming out of her canvas bag, she leaned forwards over the top of the bag and then I saw her flick the switch.

It all happened so quickly.

The bomb that she'd made that was in the black canvas bag exploded, and with it, so did Morgan.

One second, she was there and then the very next second, she wasn't.

I don't know how to say what it was that I saw, apart from to say that she was there one second, and then not there the next.

There was shattered glass and fire.

There were hungry shoppers holding their bodies in strange positions. Hungry shoppers both standing on the ground and lying on the ground holding their bodies in strange positions.

The extract from a letter written by Morgan:

'I do not know if the tape recorder and my special black handbag will have remained after I have gone. I am not as skilled at these things as my father was. Just in case they disappeared along with me, here are some words to set the record straight.

On the tape I say, and I continue to say over and over again, 'I think it will always be like this, and I therefore want no part of it anymore. I did try to make a difference and one can only try, until one makes no difference at all.'

In the handbag, there are photographs of my father in his hard hat doing what he did in those various sites around the world.

In the handbag, there is that peacock feather earring which you will remember because of course you wrote a story about it didn't you?

There is also that thick pony-tail hank of my hair which I asked you one day to cut from my head.

Do you remember?

I was making a piece of work in a church at the time, the same church in which the two of us got married.

You probably don't remember why I asked you to cut my hair, but don't worry.

I do forgive you.

You remember the church though, don't you?

You were helping me one day to move things around in the church when that poor ginger haired boy wandered in from the road. You have never learned how to deal with people like him have you?

But I forgive you all the same.

I remember one of the things that you said about that church though.

You made a point of saying that you would be happy to marry there, because the windows in the church were all clear glass. None of the windows were stained with images of Gods friends and colleagues which you felt really reassured by. You said that because of this:

If there was a real God, then he would be able to find his way into the building to bless our wedding, without having to push his way past all those man-made friends of his.

You have always had some funny ideas about God, but I suppose that this is because you only and ever wrote stories for children.

I hope that you don't find this hurtful.

Anyway, my pony-tail hank of hair.

If it is still around, please put it in the empty glass decanter that sits on that south facing windowsill next to my father's ashes and the ashes of my mother's letters.

I wonder what my father will think of what I've done.

There is one other photograph in my special black leather handbag.

It is a photograph:

Of objects on a circular mahogany tray.
Objects such as coins, a small hill of salt and an egg.
A cork, a penknife and a pair of spectacles.
There's a marble, a shell and a clothes peg.
A paper clip and a cocktail stick.
There's a cheap silver ring of no consequence and a porcelain teacup.
There are scissors and an HB pencil with a perfectly sharpened point.
And there's a pink bus ticket for a journey that I made some years ago to attend my father's funeral.

I like that photograph.

I like that photograph very much.'
K L xxx'

Pissing

I have taken to pissing in the garden, because I can't be arsed to go upstairs and do the same.

I realise that this might be the start of something that I can't stop, something that turns into other lazy-arsed things rapidly, but pissing in the garden is good for me right now.

What's it about?

When and how did it start, and when and how will it stop?

What is it about in itself, beyond the simple act of pissing in the garden?

Well?

I have a whole load of made-up jig saw maps of various parts of the world in the toilet in my house. Sealed in sticky backed clear plastic and nailed to the walls with big fancy designer silver round-headed nails. That's the kind of wanker that I am - to have such things in my house. I like to travel in my head, whilst I'm going about my business.

But this has nothing to do with the pissing in the garden trend, that has recently set in with me, as far as I am concerned.

I remember employing a pair of binoculars and drawing these close to my eyes out of a back bedroom window to view my ex-wife's body, as she sunbathed naked at the bottom of 'our' garden.

There is a little ginger-haired girl, with bright blue eyes, no older than eight, if she's a day, who lives three doors down from me. Every so often, she plays 'Knock Down Ginger' on my front door, and I am sickened by the notion of ginger being included within both her and the name of this teasing game played to what end by her at my front door I wonder?

I notice that the old man next door no longer comes out into the light, as he used to do frequently, to chat and tend his show-worthy collection of orchids living vividly within his greenhouse. His brother, whom he lives with says that 'Orchid Man', as he calls him, will probably never see the light of day again due to health issues. He uses the word 'issues' to cover I don't know what turgid range of disease his own brother now suffers from at ninety and more years of age. Will J put R out of his old misery, when the smell in the house gets too bad, I wonder, and if he does, bearing in mind the regular visits from R's GP, will J be forced if he does murder his brother to invent some elaborate story of R's sudden leaving for foreign airy shores to recuperate in a less inclement climate?

Maybe I am pissing in the garden now because unpleasant thoughts are occurring to me about people on my own doorstep.

No, but that is not it.

I knew an old woman once, who described me as a blade of grass blowing back and forth in the wind. This was all that she said to me and blamed her lack of anything else in terms of words, due to the language barrier between English and German.

I knew a woman who was covered in moles - moles breading on her body like barnacles clung to a ship. They weren't protruding moles however and we both liked the darkness and I loved her in a strange kind of way, so it was just in the light that I felt a bit strange about her.

I knew a woman who was white, who wanted to be black, and she said to me, if you were black and not white, then you would be perfect for me. I remember really struggling to understand this, and so simply went off to feed my goldfish and my silverfish that had been swimming together quite happily for years.

The black/white confused woman that I have just spoken about had a divided body, top and bottom. A perfect upper body, with a beautiful face, neck, shoulders, arms, breasts, stomach, waist and back and arse and fanny to die for, but thick veiny legs, swollen knees, and thick ankles, but then again lovely feet and toes.

She is not the reason that I am now pissing in the garden, and yet?

I played a game called 'Corridor' with some friends recently. It's a corker when playing with friends if you want to know if they are friends or not. You build corridors on a board to hem opponents in with at a whim, so that if unfortunate and hemmed in, you spend the rest of the game wandering around aimlessly amongst corridors, knowing full well that you can't win and yet being able to clearly see the person that is winning, and will eventually win.

I knew a man who had six toes on one foot - for all I know he still has these same six toes on the one foot and for all I know, he is still as happy as he always was.

My answer phone has been temperamental of late. I receive messages that seem like they may have been spoken from the bottom of an ocean somewhere.

I am pissing in the wind.

I have curtains within the downstairs area of my house that are of different lengths. Each of them has been washed separately over the years, and they have shrunk or not, according to this arbitrary washing regime. I have to say that I am ashamed of this fact, but equally proud that no guests have ever commented upon it.

Who says that pissing in the garden is a problem?

I met this man who was suggesting to me, and others present, that his idea for a film had been stolen and made into a multi-million-dollar blockbuster. But then he was a hippy and couldn't comprehend that somebody else might have had his idea before him. God bless the belief that hippies have within themselves.

I don't imagine that hippies give themselves grief about pissing in their gardens.

The radiators in my house are beginning to leak - not all of them, but just some of them.

There is a little rubber plant in my sitting room that I have cared for dearly for the last year that has, over recent weeks, begun to wane and decide for something else, other than being alive alongside me. I cannot understand it, since everything else that is a plant in my house is doing just tickety-boo. Ah, fuck the rubber plant for its lack of staying power.

I know a little ditty and it is very short.
'I like pissing in the garden
Because?'

The arses of the chairs in my sitting room are growing brittle and over time falling out. Perhaps I should stand up more often, rather than sit.

There is a young man, who walks along the main road near to my house, that I spot at least three or four times a week. He looks like a special case of one sort or another, though I am never sure and indeed, am not sure what kind of special case he might be. I don't really care, in actual fact, because I find him fascinating. He always has electrical wire and bits and pieces of electrical shit hanging out of a copious number of plastic bags that are strung from his arms. The weight of them almost makes his hands bleed. His hands are white knuckled with the weight of his treasures. What the fuck does he do with it all though? Maybe he has got a fancy apartment near to me, where everything in his house is wired up. Who knows? Who cares? What is important, is that he carries these bags of electrical crap back with him from wherever, day in day out, with some kind of idea in mind about their use, even if he never gets his shit together to actually make them into something.

I walked down the road today, and in a downstairs flat, just along from my house, all of the windows of this downstairs flat, occupied by a schizoid Scotsman senior citizen, have been smashed, but I can see him pottering about with his plants on the windowsills of his sitting room and kitchen. It is February and Mr Old Scot is blue with cold but is still tending to what he considers needs to be tended too. God love him.

I know a woman that rubs her face constantly, in the hope that she will be able to rub away the things about it that she dislikes. And yet she is beautiful in my opinion.

I know a man that is a wanker.

I know a person that has webbed feet.

I know that if I stick a thermometer up my arse, it probably won't read true right at the minute.

But do I know why I piss in the garden late at night, when I think that nobody else is looking or cares?

I have a short friend who is always short with me.

I have a tall friend who is equally short with me.

I have a middle-sized friend who is always probing and asks

questions that I will either ignore or deflect from answering until another time.

I piss in the garden, in the wind.

Maybe I just piss in the wind?

I was talking to a very good friend recently, who is a writer, and a good one at that, and the previous week had gone dry on where to take his latest short story next. He said to me that he had drunk a bottle of gin, having reached this impasse and that as a result and due to writing in his pissed state, had managed to write himself out of this dry state in terms of his narrative and break the back of the story in a fantastic fashion. I asked him if he ever pissed in the garden because he couldn't be arsed to do so in the appropriate place, and he just said no, that this had never occurred to him. He said to me, 'I assume that that is a rhetorical question?' and I put the phone down at that point, because I was busting for a whiz.

I like the smell of chives freshly cut from the garden. I like the smell of Black African music in the morning, whatever the fuck that means.

I like paying lip service to reality.

A very old friend, older than the wind, recently shaved his head for a cancer related charity, having been a hippy with long wispy hair for 24 years as he was proud to announce. The event raised large amounts for the said charity, and he looks better than he has ever done, certainly looks better than he has done for the past twenty-four years. Ho hum.

I knew a man some years ago, who turned trees upside down for a living. RF was a dark and troubled soul, who loved forests - preferred trees to people, I am certain. RF was a man of few words, but of extraordinary actions. He never looked physically capable of creating the things that he made. He had inherited money as a young man, and a not insubstantial sum at that. Enough to ensure that if he couldn't be arsed, he would never need to work throughout his life to support himself. As a child, he had had a thing about trees. Climbing them, making elaborate camps and pseudo houses in them, and under them, out of whatever scrap materials he could muster by begging, borrowing, or stealing. As a teenager, he would travel to forests, far and wide, in search of trees that he could have elaborate imaginings about in terms of what they might look like as a house, if they were cut down carefully, with their branch spans methodically plotted, transported elsewhere and then turned upside down, rebuilt exactly as they had been when heading for the sky, but now heading for the earth instead, somewhere else in the world, and then built around - walled in, between their arms of branches. Space for windows here and there, for a door or doors. A house, summerhouse, greenhouse, studio, a space for whatever, made out of an enormous tree that has simply been turned upside down. And then suddenly, as if this was his God given right, he was granted an inheritance which meant that he could travel to forests now, far and wide, and no longer simply imagine, but now buy an enormous tree of his choosing, have it cut down with mathematical precision, transported to wherever, put it back together piece by piece, but upside down and create something differently beautiful to the thing that it had originally been, either for himself of for a fat cat patron who just wanted one of RF's things on their land.

I got a letter from his brother recently, to say that RF had been killed in a car accident. RF was crouching down, by the side of a road, in the dark apparently, somewhere, anywhere – it's not important, looking at an enormous tree that he had wanted to buy, cut down, transport, and turn into a chapel for a wealthy religious patron of his.

RF's brother said that he had visited the scene in daylight, the day after his brothers' death. He stressed to me in his letter how stunningly beautiful the tree was that his brother was looking at when the fatal collision took place. The driver of the car that ran RF down was a writer it was later revealed in the local press. The writers' wife gave evidence in mitigation at the trial, that her partner had written three quarters of a novel and had got stuck with where to go next. On the night that the writer ran RF down, the writer was, according to his wife, just popping out for a drive in the night to collect his thoughts.

She also said that in the weeks leading up to this fated car journey, her husband had taken to urinating in the garden because, for some reason, he couldn't be arsed to go upstairs in the house and do the same.

Things Not Worth Keeping

Please describe the 'thing' that you would like to nominate for the Millennium Collection of things not worth keeping - remember that the thing must be an actual thing that is yours to keep.

I came across 'it' - my 'thing' - recently, having forgotten that 'it' was there.

'It' was screwed into the bottom of a drawer that is part of a chest of drawers that otherwise contains my underwear and: some startlingly loud sets of trouser braces from the 1970's which I recall at the time wearing with pride; a pink bow tie which I have only ever worn when feeling the need to look ridiculous; some old squash balls of the yellow spot kind that have been thrashed around white walled rooms in the past to help me in maintaining a certain level of fitness; a small plastic bag from a Dublin jewellers shop, containing a receipt for 'Gents and Ladies' wedding rings.

'It' is a full crown tooth, complete with its own specially designed screw thread post, that at one time was screwed into my lower jaw. You are welcome to have it, complete in its new setting – i.e., screwed into the drawer - if you so wish.

Why is this thing not worth keeping? It's a long story, but I'll be as short as I can in telling it.

As a young teenager, I had a full complement of teeth in my head, and was often complimented about the quality of this full complement: about their shape their evenness

their whiteness

and about the handsome contribution that they made towards my smile, whenever I smiled.

At the age of sixteen, I left school and started work for an insurance company.

I bought a slate grey three-piece suit to mark the occasion, and to wear day in day out at work from then on, until it wore out.

I bought a gold pocket watch with a fob, which graced the right-hand pocket of my waistcoat.

To accompany me on my first day at work, I also bought a packet of twenty Dunhill cigarettes, and two packets of Polos.

The suit, the watch with fob, and the cigarettes, would help me to look the business I thought. A big part of being successful in this insurance business would be about looking the business I thought.

I knew that I would find it difficult to get used to the taste of tobacco smoke on my tongue - hence the packets of Polos. These would, I thought, be some insurance against the decimation of my tongue, and would also ensure fresh breath, at all times. They assisted in neither of these aims, as they clearly had other aims of their own.

I became addicted to tobacco, and in my vain attempts to stave off the torrid tastes and smells that it breeds, I became addicted to Polos as well. Twenty Dunhill and a packet of Polos went hand in hand as a daily order at the local newsagents, for the next ten years.

My teeth were beautiful, until I let Rowntree MacIntosh begin work on them.

A fag and a Polo together.

Two Polos first, and then a fag.

A Polo, a fag, and then another Polo, to finish nicely.

'Fag, fag, Polo, fag, Polo, fag. Polo fag, Fag fag, Polo, fag, Polo, Polo fag!!!'

Polo. The mint with the hole. It had its own hole, and as I was very soon to find out, was very effective at reproducing holes in the things within me that it spent most of its time close to. My teeth.

I have always dreaded the dentists. I dread pain. I'm not good with it. It fuckin hurts. It shouldn't be allowed.

'The tooth is the only part of the sentient body that we fear and consider it normal to lose.'

By David Kunzle, from - The Art of Pulling Teeth in the Seventeenth and Nineteenth Centuries: From Public Martyrdom to Private Nightmare and Political Struggle? Fragments for a History of the Human Body - Part Three

David Kunzle - smart arse!

Until the Polo 'plague' began to spread within me, dental visits had always been of the 'check-up' variety - a quick prod all round, and then the thankful thumbs up and a cheerful waiving away for another six months.

Even these 'check ups' though, I found to be a painful ordeal. My dentist was Scottish. He had a rich regional accent and to my shame, I could never understand a word or phrase that he said apart from, 'Av a rinz young man'.

He practiced his art from an old Masonic Hall. A dark place. Always cold. Leaded windows. Lots of stained glass. Wooden floors, that looked like they had been coated with dark maple syrup.

My dentist shared a floor in this Masonic Hall with a female chiropodist - a strange pairing of professions, I thought at the time. I still think this now. Her 'surgery' was part of his dentists waiting room, and the delicate art that she practised was separated from the likes of me, waiting for my teeth to be seen to, by the flimsiest of what I remember now to be a long white shower curtain. Yes, that's exactly what it was, a fuckin shower curtain.

I would sit and wait, dipping into such magazine delights as, 'The Lady' and 'Inexpensive Yachting For All', during which time old men and elderly women would disappear behind this shower curtain. They would talk about their feet and the various troubles that they were having with them, and then there would be a sequence of loud clipping sounds, followed sometimes by grunts and moans and sometimes by sighs of relief and joy.

Sometimes, the curtain would be pulled back, whilst the chiropodist popped out for something, and the strangest configurations of feet and toes would then be available for a moments viewing, until the good lady returned, new sterilised and horrendous looking tools in hand, to complete whatever nasty business she had earlier begun.

I have to say that these experiences were disgusting. I didn't like dentists, but I have to say that I liked the fact that my dentist gave house room to this foot woman even less. What she did, the conversations that I heard her having with various old folk, and the mutant feet that she handled on a day-to-day basis made me nauseous, gave me nightmares, stopped me going to the dentists - until it was too late.

I let Rowntree MacIntosh claim a victory over my teeth. The bastards. I remember wondering if they and my Scottish dentist might be working in cahoots to rid me of my teeth.

I am good at meeting deadlines, but only if these are imposed from an exterior perspective - I am not good at creating them for myself. I never have been. I have always left things until the last possible moment.

I am certain, with the benefit of hindsight, that my Scottish dentist must have presented me with a series of verbal deadlines in relation to the death of my teeth, though amidst the rich regional accent that he possessed which I have already mentioned, I must not have heard the various well-informed predictions that he cast in my direction about them. I missed appointments, because I didn't hear them in deadline terms, and thought that all would continue to be well, because I hadn't heard my dentist say that things would not in fact be well, or perhaps I did hear him well enough, but chose simply to ignore the truth. My confused perspective upon deadlines and my responsibility and commitment towards them is revealed here for the sham that it is.

Over time, it all very rapidly turned to shit. My teeth hit the fan thanks to some considerable help from Rowntree MacIntosh, and my own inability to properly grasp that some deadlines do indeed result in exactly that if they are not met - a deadline, or in my case, a dead tooth or dead teeth.

Words and phrases quickly followed that I'm sure David Kunzle - who is quoted above - became more than familiar with during the research for his very informative and wide-ranging essay.

'I am not sure that I can do anything to save this one now.'

'An X ray is going to be necessary here, in order to discover the state of play beneath this one young man.'

'Root filling.'

'Extraction is our only option here. I am so sorry.'

'Please squeeze my arm young man, if any of the following fifteen injections that I need to administer, causes you any pain.'

'You see, the nerve that serves this tooth has just let you know that it is there, that's all. There is nothing to be concerned about. This is all perfectly natural.'

'Just hang on there a moment, I'll need to get a second opinion about this.'

'Yes, I can save this one, in a manner of speaking, by screwing a replacement tooth into your lower jaw into what's left of the root for the original tooth that you have let go.'

'I'll be needing to see you at least once a week if not twice over the next six to eight weeks or so, if we're to successfully get on top of the problems that we both know are facing us here.'

'We can follow this direction together, though the NHS subsidy towards treatment of this kind is rare, and only sanctioned in special cases. I'm not sure that you would be viewed as special in their eyes I have to say, in which case there would be a rather large matter of payment involved, and I'd also say that I cannot, in your case, guarantee a successful outcome. You'll need to commit to having the work done and paying for it before we can discover whether it is in fact going to ultimately be successful.'

'I'm sorry to be so harsh on your pocket, without also being able to guarantee a positive outcome.

And so, a number of jobs were done, some of them well, and some of them not so well, and one of them badly.

I could have bought a good second-hand car, or paid for a decent holiday somewhere hot, with the money that I spent on the treatment connected with the 'crown tooth' that is now screwed into the bottom of a drawer in my bedroom.

In offering this to you, in giving it away, in the process of thinking about giving it to you, in the act of writing about it, I have returned to some times and some places and some people that, were it not for your project, I would probably not have ever returned to.

I don't now need the tooth itself to, for example, return to that Masonic Hall again, and recall in more detail what was there; to pursue the significance or otherwise that the six dentists that I have had over the course of my life have all been Scottish; to try and remember the circumstances surrounding the loss of the watch and fob that I mention, which I at one time cherished, but now no longer possess; to examine in a bit more detail why I am so appalling in real terms at meeting deadlines, including the one that you have set for your project – 'Postcards must be returned to us by January 31st.' - it is today the 6th February, as I continue to write here.

I don't need 'it' anymore. 'Its' yours.

The Shape Of Things

[I]

I remember a time. In nineteen sixty-nine. When we were:

Sitting together. Sitting in the sitting room together. Sitting in the sitting room together, almost in the dark. There were those lovely dense and heavy lined shit-brown nylon curtains that had given up swishing, pulled not quite fully together, across the sitting room window. There was a thin stark corridor of yellowed light streaming through the brittle 'nets' in the available gap. A light that cut across the carpeted sitting room floor, across the flesh-coloured raise-tiled fire-place base, up across a tacky little fake coal-fire gas-fire, further up to large brown swirls on the embossed wallpaper that decorated the chimney breast, on its way dissecting in two a framed watercolour painting by a local artist with little or no talent and not at all local to where we were then. A watercolour of a Cornish harbour hard at work, at a time when there were enough fish around to make the building of a harbour worthwhile.

We were together, father and son. Sitting together in our sitting room. Sitting on opposite sides of the room from one another, our sides, our halves of the room, divided by a hatchet of light that split the darkness of the room in two. We were waiting together silently because......my father had said that it wasn't quite time, not quite, it wasn't bang-on according to his watch, not exactly the time that it needed to be, and until it was, we must resign ourselves to simply sitting and waiting and occupying our minds with something else. That was so very easy for him to say, because excitement wasn't boiling then inside of him, like it was inside of me. Excitement for what might happen next in the world.

I looked at him across the room, my father, the little broken fragments that I could see of him anyway through the rooms strange haze. He was checking his watch, now and again, counting down the minutes and seconds, occupying himself like a true trooper.

And what was I doing? I was just trying to get comfortable in my brown nylon armchair. I was making the shape of a large zero with my bare arms, so that these followed the circular line of the armchair's arms, which were like two wide semi circles that started at each of my shoulders, curved outwards, and then met back again at the outside of both my knees. If the surface of these two six-inch nylon covered wooden semi circles had been flat, that would have been fine, but they weren't. Their outer edge led back into the seat base of the chair at about a forty-five-degree angle, so in order to let my arms extend fully out along their line, and as well allow for this ridiculous angle, I had to lock my shoulders rigid, and lock again at the elbows and wrists like a broken armed tractioned patient. This brown nylon sitting room suite wasn't a comfortable brown nylon sitting room suite. Even if I were to stretch my imagination, the word comfortable wouldn't be found there anywhere, not even rattling about lonely as a cloud.

My father was thinking about time as time was passing and I was thinking about design. Or, more specifically, bad design. That's what I was occupying my head with whilst I was waiting for him to give the thumbs up.

And then somebody opened the sitting room door, and the light from our bright sunlit hallway charged into the room revealing me with my robotic extensions looking as comfortable as a cow's leg on a butcher's block. Whoever that somebody was didn't say anything, and they shut the door as quickly as they had opened it, returning us to where we just were. Or not quite. During this little distraction, my father had obviously stretched himself out in his chair and had pushed his legs further out across the floor. In the thin strip of light that cut across the sitting room carpet, there was now a pair of slippers. I say a pair of slippers, but only because I could also see evidence of my fathers socked ankles going into them. The slippers themselves, the material they were made from, the colour combination and pattern on them, matched the carpet that they were resting on. Exactly. My father had a pair of brown wool and worsted chameleons on his feet.

I was old before I was young. Though half my life is over now, the same thing seems still to apply. At ten years old, the world and many of the things in it occupied my head in strange ways much more frequently than those same things ever occupied my body.

Carpets and slippers in a dark sitting room in nineteen sixty-nine. At ten years old, I occupied myself thinking which came first, the carpet or the slippers. I occupied myself thinking about the nature of the mind of the man or woman designer as they might have attempted to sell this concept of carpet and slipper harmony to a broad-minded marketing team. I thought about what an earnest selling presentation this must have been, about the props that might have been used during such a presentation. I thought about whether my father really valued the fact that his slippers matched the carpet exactly. A child who is old before he is young occupies himself in this way.

And now I think back to something that happened on the end of my finger in that dark sitting room, sitting there with my dad. It happened whilst I was concentrating on the slippers and their place in the wider scheme of things. The end of my finger. A badge. That badge pin. Fiddling with this while concentrating on something else. I jammed the badge pin into the end of my finger. A little fountain of pain. I got up and out of my nylon armchair and pushed my badge hand into the shaft of light just down the road from my father's chameleons. It didn't look right. The badge pin carrying the badge, embedded in the soft fleshy top of my middle finger. The pin and the badge were great reflectors of light though. I remember swivelling the badge finger around and about and watching for the little satellites of colour to cross the walls of the dark room which they did very nicely thank you.

After a while, and when eventually my father noticed what was going on and told me to stop being so ridiculous, I pulled the badge pin out of my finger and pressed the end of the finger with a thumb to see what would happen. A beautifully perfect miniature sphere of vermilion blood rose out from inside of me and came to rest over the top of the hole in my finger.

The blood was from blood group O. I knew this because I had once asked my father about the whole blood group business, and he had given me the good news about there being plenty of mine around in the event of a major accident. It was good to know things like this from an early age. Stopped you fearing the worst when you came off your bike on a concrete path, or if a chisel slipped when you were helping your father in the shed, or if when you were throwing flat stones at a group of seagulls in the sky with a group of small friends and the friend that was standing behind you was a lousy thrower and one of his flat stones misfired into the back of your head and the walk home was going to take half an hour at least.

I remember my father suddenly saying from out of that sitting room darkness, him saying that the time was suddenly right. At last. He said switch it on then and let's see. I could hear the excitement rising in his voice in those seconds, though he wasn't willing to go overboard with it right at that moment.

Every day, during the previous few weeks, he'd been telling me that what we were just about to see was something that he dreamed about as a child. That he had read about this in comics. That he'd consumed comic picture after comic picture of it week by week when he was a child, and then he'd dreamt about it in the night.

He said switch it on then, but he was really talking to himself, reminding himself that this was what needed to be done. Thinking aloud. He did this a lot, and sometimes it was very confusing, because there were times when he did actually mean for me to do something. Sometimes his thinking aloud was not just for himself exclusively. But I didn't know the rules of when it was him and when it was me. I remember thinking that I must remind myself to ask him about this when I'm older, and I also remember wondering then whether I would actually be able to remember to remember in the future.

I never wondered about the moon in the way that my father did. Of course, it was exciting, but I never wondered about it. I wondered about the future. About what it would look like. About what I would look like. About what my father would look like. My father has been wondering about the moon since he was a child.

On. On. On. On. On. On. On. On at last. Thank goodness. The television screen spewed its own special light from its little corner of plenty in the room. A hideout in America was suddenly in front of us. NASA. Mission Control, 20th July 1969. What we were about to see had happened during the night before, whilst we were sleeping. Well, I know that I was sleeping, but I'm not certain about my father. Perhaps he was laying there with one, or even two eyes open, thinking about Michael Collins, Edwin Aldrin, and Neil Armstrong, and feeling envious as hell.

What did we see first? Hundreds of men and just a few women, busy as busy can be, in front of computer screens. It was clearly as hot as hell where they were. There were lots of rolled up shirt sleeves and ties unbuttoned at the collar. Everybody seemed to be wearing spectacles. Thinking a man onto the moon obviously had a knock-on effect where the eyesight was concerned. They were going to put this man on the moon in just a very few minutes.

My father looked frightened, excited, nervous. He was completely transfixed. It was almost as if he was there hovering above the moon himself, when in fact he was simply sitting in his sitting room with me.

My father had an opinion in the darkness about Michael Collins which he shared with me. He said that he felt very sorry for Michael. Said that Michael must have realised even then that his would be the one name of the three names that in the future people would find it most difficult to remember. And why? Well, because of course Michael wasn't actually going to do it - stand on the moon that is. Michael had to keep the engine running on the mother ship whilst the other two boys got to go and play on the moon.

I remember thinking, whilst I was watching, about what Michael might actually have been thinking. I wondered if he might be thinking about immortality and how he might achieve it. He could fuck up on purpose and leave his colleagues on the moon to die. That would be a scoop. After all the training, his jealousy gets the better of him. Michael rows the boat back home - on his own.

There was much 'T minusing', and then the Eagle had landed and then, after a while, there was a man on the moon. Billions of good dollars to get one man to a place where he couldn't breathe, where there was no water, where he couldn't grow anything to eat, but where he could beat the world long jump record without having to try very hard at all. Billions of good dollars for one man to go to the moon, just because it was there.

My father dreamed about the impossibility of a man making this journey when he was a child, and now he could actually see it for himself, sitting in his sitting room, sitting in his sitting room together with his son.

Billions of dollars forced into thought and design. One man, or a group of men - with maybe just a few women - saying we want to call it the Eagle for obvious reasons and reasons with which everyone will agree. It will look like this, and the two men in it will look like this etc.

I remember looking at the Eagle. I remember looking at Neil and Edwin - Edwin better known as Buzz. None of it looked like it should be where it was. Who decided that the moon deserved us looking like that? Interesting that those thinkers, those designers, decided that if a man should be in a place where he wouldn't naturally be, then perhaps better to draw attention to this fact, to exaggerate this fact, rather than attempt thoughts and designs that make the machine and the man blend harmoniously with the surroundings. Let's admit that we shouldn't be there shall we, and let's make that clear for everyone to see. And let's put a man on the moon with the initials NA, and hope that no one sees the possibility of NOT APPLICABLE in them.

As soon as it was over, it was over. My father's dreams had come true. Push the button son, he said.

That was it.

I pushed the button, and the light from the television screen was vacuumed back into the machine, leaving a tiny white circle at the exact centre of the screen. Televisions don't do this anymore do they. Some designers must have found this little white dot irritating, I suppose. But they used to do it then. Funny to miss something like that, a little dot, but I do. A tiny white full moon at the centre of a black rectangle. It was there. It was still there. It was just about still there. Now you see it, now you don't. Oh. All gone. Ah. Silence.

My father sat in the darkness. The wind had been taken from his sails. His Push the button son, was like a sad and sorry winded instruction. His dreams were all washed away in the dark.

In the silence, I wondered what my father would now dream about into the future. What would he imagine to be the next impossible thing, and how long would it take in his lifetime before this same thing became possible? What had the Eagle landing done for his dreams?

We sat together in the sitting room, after this one small step for a man, both occupying our minds. I didn't say anything and neither did my father. I heard him move. The sitting room door opened. Light poured into the room from the sunlit hallway again. My father was leaving the room, but I didn't watch him. I watched his collapsed shadow cast across the sitting room floor as it moved through the doorway to follow him out of the room. The shadow shut the door behind itself. I remember thinking that I must remember when I'm older to ask my father what he was thinking as we sat there in the dark occupying our minds and also what he was feeling as he left the room. I'm sure these thoughts and feelings were not NOT APPLICABLE.

On my own then, at ten years old, in that sitting room in July 1969, with my father's broken dream hanging in the air. I got to thinking in a backwards and forwards way about the shape that things were, the shape that they are, and the shape of things to come. Old before I was young, ha ha! Pulling my young head around up and down history, sitting in the dark with a punctured finger.

Where to start? Well, I started at the beginning with the wheel of course. That seemed as good a place as any. Yes.

And these were the things that I thought:

Now I knew, because I had been told this, that nobody knew the exact date and time for the invention of the wheel. Strange to think that a fact as significant as that wasn't dragged carefully through history so that we could all know and perhaps celebrate it annually.

All those men and woman from the past, fumbling around on the ground for centuries, at their own very human pace. All that time spent looking up at the day and night-time sky in fear, in worship. In fear and worship of two circles, one of which had the power to change its shape as the month moved on.

Easy to say that there had always been wheels in the sky. Models to make a chariot charge through the dust, or a penny farthing hop the cobbles. I wondered when it was that we had clicked. When a man - because it probably would have been, but only perhaps at his wife's insistent suggestion - tore the shape A4of these circles out of the sky and applied them to a piece of rock or wood, so that the two of them could begin to defy gravity in the very first degree. I was sure that the idea for the wheel had come out of the sky, when common sense had got the better of worship and fear.

Perhaps unconsciously, all those centuries and centuries and centuries and centuries later, we sent men to the moon in order to say thank you to it, the moon, for the idea of the wheel that in the beginning had helped us eventually to get to the moon. A grateful circle of gratitude inscribed by the shape of the moon itself at certain times. Here are some men and some extremely expensive bits and pieces of the highest technology for you moon, to say thank you for the wheel. A strange expensive and elaborate ceremony of worship actually on site. What a gift moon. Eh!! Just another circle in thought and deed.

On my own, in that dark sitting room that my father had just left, I got to thinking also about words as well. This circle worship had found its way very neatly into some of our biggest words that cover pages and fly out of mouths in the West. Words like:

God.

Mother.

Power.

Love.

And the word Moon, it had two circles, which was of course only right, given its special place in history. It was there in 'Old' right at the beginning, because it suggested quite correctly that our time was almost up. A circle here and a circle there, all littered about for comfort. But these circles were not to be found in Life or Here or Death, funnily enough.

What wonderful things to be thinking, at aged ten, in 1969!

Now, at the age of thirty-seven, I think about a time again, and about the shape of things. Sitting with my own son, in our very different sitting room. I think now, whilst he's here with me, about a time that hasn't happened yet. The year 2000. I wonder what this future will look like and I'm not the only one. It's another benchmark for man, the extravagant celebration of it handed down to me and everybody else through history.

The year 2000. Christ, there are three circles in it, so of course it's bound to be something massive. Just has to be, doesn't it? But let's just hold it there, two and three zeros hanging in the air, because right now it's only...

... 1995 going on 1996. The moon has been abandoned in favour of better fare. Jupiter and the Sun. People with bottomless purses sent a Galileo named craft off to Jupiter to discover an atmosphere that does what it does 600 million miles from here. Galileo would be proud, I'm sure. They sent it a while ago, but its only just arrived, hence all the latest fuss. The same has already been done for Mars and Venus in the past apparently, but I must have missed this in the thin science newspaper columns years back. Thin columns such as these always contain sums of money beyond the imagination. $2000,000,000. A set of figures almost as wide as the column that contains it. We love our circles don't we, and the more the merrier it seems. Hey Ho!

These same people with the bottomless bottomless purses have just sent a SOHO to our lovely Sun. The Solar and Heliospheric Observatory - a peep show, with our lovely Sun as the innocent performer. An unerotic dance up there in the heavens. They want to know about its core and corona but will probably get their fingers burnt in the process. Hey Ho! $1000,000,000.

Just a thought this: that we've managed to rip a hole in the O zone, perhaps so that we can see the lovely Sun just that little bit better, and now, at a modest cost, SOHOs off to warm the cockles of its own heart on our behalf. Hey Ho!

But now to the future. Let's bring our two and three zeros out of the air and back to the earth for a long hard stare because:

There they are, grandfather, father, and son, three men in the future, sitting in the future together, in a room in a London skyscraper. A hotel room hired for the night of December 31st, 1999, by the father. Three beds in a room. A room for the grandfather, for the father, and for the father's son, a son who has so much to live for, though neither grandfather nor father are able to tell the son what this so much might be.

The room itself is unremarkable, other than the fact that its way up in the sky. The three of them defying gravity, with the aid of iron and concrete. There are thick but unremarkable curtains closed tightly across the one large window that the room contains.

In the night the three of them attempt to sleep peacefully, but to no avail. Six eyes wide open and searching in the dark. In the night, they imagine the scenes that they might witness as the sun appears in the morning:

A metropolis of crystal towers, gleaming globular monorails and sleek streamlined space buses coming gently to a halt on immaculate heliports. Orderly peaceful smiling groups of city dwellers in colourful suits exchanging pleasantries amongst the wide tree and plant lined malls, a wonderful freshness to the air filling a thousand nostrils here and there.

Six eyes in the dark searching for the detail that tomorrow will bring. Hey Ho!
On. On. On. On. On. On. On. On. On. On. Before they all know it, the alarm clock is on, bleeping them inE1to the day. Here it is everyone, just the other side of those unremarkable curtains.

The father is up first, fresh as a daisy, in spite of his wide eyes in the night. The grandfather, so very old he is now, reaches for those thick dense lensed glasses that simply help him to see the world in a haze, rather than not to see it at all. The son gingerly slips onto his own head a virtual reality helmet - a prized Xmas gift - then says switch it on dad, and dad dutifully does what he's told. Beneath the shiny black plastic arcade that shields the sons' eyes from the room, and from his two genetic kin, a smile appears on the boy's face. He feels at home and safe and excited in that town or city or world called Pixilated.

The father looks at the grandfather, who sits at the end of one of the beds, his legs extending to the floor, elbows on his knees, resting his chin in cupped hands. The father looks at the son who sits on the end of another bed, his legs hanging over its edge, his fingers pressing buttons on a handset to make things take shape in Pixilated. The father walks to a mirror hanging on one of the walls of the room. The father looks at himself. The father walks to a table by one of the beds in the room and switches on a television that stands on the table. Just as the picture appears, the father notices the grandfathers brown patterned slippered feet resting uncertainly on the bright yellow carpet that covers the hotel rooms floor. The father notices the sons' feet falling out of green pyjama trousers, bare and dangling in the air above the yellow carpet out over the edge of the bed. The father looks down to his own feet and smiles at his bright yellow slippers.

There is a picture on the television screen. It's a picture of the planet earth taken from outer space. The father moves towards the curtains at the bedroom window. It's the morning of January 1st in the year 2000. He pulls the curtains open and stands there looking. There is:

A metropolis of crystal towers, gleaming globular monorails and sleek streamlined space buses coming gently to a halt on immaculate heliports. Orderly peaceful smiling groups of city dwellers in colourful suits are exchanging pleasantries amongst the wide tree and plant lined malls, a wonderful freshness to the air filling a thousand nostrils here and there.

This scene has been carefully painted by a talented artist, with a not very vivid imagination, onto a set of blinds that those thick curtains at the window were hiding.

The father leads the grandfather across to the blinds, and the grandfather squints into the picture before him. He says good for you son, I'm glad for you that things have turned out as you imagined that they would. Can I go now, because?:

Do you remember when we sat together all those years ago, and I felt very sorry for Michael Collins. Well, since then, I've thought a lot about the sun. That's been mainly on my mind. You remember a few years ago that they sent that SOHO thing up and out to have a look at it. Well, I heard on the radio that it's coming back today. I think that's what they said anyway. Or maybe it wasn't. I know they said it was coming back but come to think of it it wasn't today. No. Maybe it was tomorrow. Oh, fuck it, it'll come back sometime wont it. What comes around goes around. Eh son. Well, I have this theory son about that old fucker in the sky. It said on the radio that the computers on SOHO were on the verge of sending back a vital piece of information when something malfunctioned and sent SOHO itself hurtling back to earth years in advance of when it was due to return. I think it's probably coming back to tell us something important about life, don't you? And I think it might be this...

...humans are suddenly here having not been here, and then they stop being here very suddenly, having been here. I SOHO have discovered that the sun is........Well...

Here comes the sun...

Oh dear.

Oh.

O

O

o

o

o

.

.

Sixteen Spaces for Remembrance

One

Sometimes,
I imagine a child on the moon,
a child on the moon, to replace that man,
a child on the moon, and not that man,
making that first small step on behalf of us all.
How,
I wonder,
might the words of this child, be different from the words of that man?

Two

At school, during days, my son learns about time.
About the seasons.
About where dirty water goes.
About the bony inside of himself.
About how to get on with his small colleagues.
About how far one thing is   from another thing.
About what things in the world look like when he draws or paints them.
Each time he learns, he grows inside of himself, in relation to the world.
With this in mind,
I'm trying hard,
Right now,
To think about the weight of what I have learned today,

Or yesterday,

Or even the day before that, or the day before that etc etc etc.

Three

There is a bear.

There is a bicycle.

There is a man, in a very great hurry.

There is a woman arguing. There is a car.

There is a friend who needs to be got to.

There is no time to think. There is too much time to think.

There is a small child.

There are different things for different people to live with for the rest of their lives.

There is a noise that nobody wants to hear.

There is the madness of impatience.

The bear's name is Norman.

The bicycle changes shape quickly when it is hit by the car.

The small child wasn't looking properly - apart from at Norman – who'd been accidentally dropped on the pavement on the other side of the road.

Norman was a friend who needed to be got to.

The man in the car was involved in an argument with the arguing woman and the argument was about love - or rather the lack of it.

What the man and the woman would think about for the rest of their lives was marked across their faces when their car hit the bicycle ridden by the small child - a child riding to save a bear called Norman.

As this happens, there is a second woman and a second man who are suddenly childless and lost.

Four

'The face of God is probably made of light.'
I said this to a child and the child said -
'Yes it is,
Of course it is.
It is,
So don't be silly with a question about it now.'
The faith of children?

Five

When will my child begin to think these things:
How safe are my toys?
How safe is my room?
How safe is my house?
How safe is my walking?
How safe is my thinking?
How safe is my body?
How safe am I?

Six

I see the child's face first. Then the big, coloured flag on a pole that the child has holstered at its groin. The flag and pole outsize the child. The child's arms strain at the weight.

In spite of all this, the child has a smile the length of a pier across its face.

Pride and joy.

This child heads an angry crowd of grown-ups. They have their word blooded banners. They have their violent causey voices, letting out in the wind. They mean business with both, but I keep coming back to the child's face. To the possible thoughts inside the child's head.

The grown-ups are shouting for a justice to be done. It's a justice the child cannot possibly understand.

So, I imagine this child with a different flag and the child heading a crowd of children instead. The smile of pride and joy has gone. This child and these children are shouting on behalf of themselves.

Can you hear the different things that they are shouting?

Seven

Marriage is a wonderful idea, until it sometimes breaks apart.

Then the children are needed to be shields.

To be barbed weapons.

To be innocent bargaining chips.

Their tears are encouraged to make a point, or their smiles are squeezed to make a point.

Who is thinking of who in these situations?

Who is protecting who in these situations?

Eight

There is a secret factory, within which, there is one large room devoted to children.

There are no toys to be found in this room though.

In fact,   there are no children.

The only evidence of children in this room is to be found in the shape of their small bodies, marked out in chalk across the surface of green and brown camouflaged uniform material that is spread out across tabletops.

There are scissors.

And there are sewing machines.

And there are threads and buttons.

Each day, a lorry in disguise, arrives to take rails full of these small uniforms out into the world.

The adults that work in this one large room, devoted to children, have little to say to one another as they go about their cutting and sewing and pressing each day.

Nine

If my child is ever lost to me, it will break me in ways that I cannot imagine.

It will break me in ways that I do not wish to imagine about.

I have a Pocket Oxford English Dictionary in which the word 'grief' sits awkwardly between the word's 'gridiron' and 'griffin'.

I notice that a gridiron is a barred metal broiling/grilling frame.

I notice that a griffin is a creature from Greek mythology with an eagle's head and wings, and a lions body.

Maybe, on reflection, the word grief is exactly where it needs to be in my pocket OED.

Ten

I have a map in front of me, but it does not show, for example, that my local children's playground has broken glass amongst the wood chip surface beneath the climbing frame.

My map also does not show the thickness of the ice at a pond nearby in wintertime.

It does not show that strange dogs are not always friendly. It does not show that in a house, water and electricity are never friendly. It does not show that in various houses, children will be beaten and bruised for simply being children. Will be fed a diet of coke and television. Will have love but little else. Will have a house that they hardly see, because of boarding school. Will wonder why they are children.

Where would children like to go? What are the possibilities for them? And where are the maps to help them find their way?

Eleven

'Thinking is only for when your eyes are closed.'

My child said this to me when, one day, I asked him what he was thinking about.

The way in which he said his 'Thinking is only for...' was said with such honesty and with such conviction, that it made me stop and think. And then I realised the trap that he'd led me into with his innocence.

Twelve

I am a human being, and I am a parent and... I will try to be....I hope that I can be....I think that I will be able to....I tell others that I have....I kid myself sometimes that I have managed to....I both cry and laugh about my child because....I talk with my child and love our conversations...I try the best that I can to....I laugh with my child even when it isn't funny...I know I make mistakes sometimes but... This or that decision is for my child's benefit, because....

My child is a human being, and my child is a child.

Thirteen

A child is floating on its back in the sea.

A blue sea.

The child is smiling and laughing.

The child's eyes so wide at the sky,

A blue sky.

Salt and water bearing the child's weight.

On the other side of the headland, from where this child is happy, a man in a balaclava rolls leaking barrels of heavy chemicals along a set of ramps from the back of a rusty Transit van, down the beach and into the sea.

Fourteen

When there are flies on a walking child's face,

in the corner of a standing child's eyes,

visiting the body of a speechless and barely moving child,

at these moments, is it not all of us that have failed in our attempt to be human?

Fifteen

Will it be worth being a child?

In two or three hundred years' time?

Sixteen

Sometimes

I imagine a child on the moon

a child on the moon to replace that man

a child on the moon and not that man

making that first small step on behalf of us all
How
I wonder
might the words of this child
be different from the words of that man

About the Author

K. Michael Weaver is a Cambridge based writer, performer, music radio DJ and a practicing Integrative Therapist. He is the founder and director of 'The K. Michael Weaver Collective Ltd' - a multi-disciplinary cross art form resource and networking agency.

He studied theatre at Dartington College of Arts, in the late 1980's. During the mid-1990's, with the experimental theatre company desperate optimists, he collaborated and performed in a trilogy of devised theatre pieces: Dedicated, Indulgence and Stalking Realness. These multi-media pieces covered issues such as: how capitalism obscures ethics; the paradoxes of freedom; notions about the real, the authentic and the genuine in our culture. The three pieces toured extensively throughout the UK and across mainland Europe to much acclaim. In 2001, he was invited to be part of Sheffield based theatre company Forced Entertainment and he collaborated and performed with them in First Night, which also toured the UK and Europe extensively, this time including as well, venues in the USA, Canada, and Australia. He worked with them again in 2004 with a re-tour of First Night and on The Travels.

He writes for the ear, rather than for the eye. In other words, all the pieces are written to be performed/read out loud, as well as simply read.

His performance writing and short stories tangle with the human condition, poking it within sometimes surreal narratives, just to see what might be there.

Man at the Window, his first published collection of works, is also available from Honeybee Books. They will also be publishing his collections Coughing Positions and She Writes Like an Angel Might Write in 2023, and then Some Sum Thoughts Over Time - a part fact, part fictive journal, and then his Collected Theatre Writings, in 2024.

He regularly performs his work live and sees this as a vital aspect of his writing/editing process and the journey of his words, prior to having them published in a written and fixed book form.

Regarding his work as a DJ, he was a regular guest presenter on Clubglobal - a world music radio show under just the name Weaver, with DJ Skunk, for six years, on Cambridge 105 Radio between 2014 and 2020.

He currently hosts his own weekly hour-long dance music show on Cambridge 105 Radio: The Groove Hour - with Weaver, playing selections from his extensive jazz tronic/jazz fusion and world jazz music collection.

He also practices as an Integrative Therapist in Cambridge and South Cambridgeshire.

Special Thanks

Thanks for every kind of support and assistance to: Olwyn Foot - my vital Editor & Text Reader, Chella Adgopul - my lovely Publisher & Designer at Honeybee Books, Ed Walker, my number 1 fan, Irene Galstian - who helps me every day to live in the moment, Bill Schwartz, Hazel Hare, Jill Eastland, Esther Foreman, Deborah Chadbourn, Nick Skelton, Kay Goodridge, Pete Monahan, Sheena Mooney, Dianne Foreman, St-John Costelloe, Rebecca Foreman, Eddie Rivero, Cathy Gomm, Cathy Dunbar, Andrew Hind, Jenny Mace, Sue Bates & Tim Smart, Connor Schwartz, Loren Parker, Nuala Schwartz and Ro, Sandra & Steve Barton, Julie Coimbra, Elspeth Owen, Matthew Springford, Mary Geddes, Gordon Warner, Miss Kitty Voget, Prof Alan Read - UCL, Tim Shuker-Yates, Jacqui Browning, Philip Boys, Avishka Don and his friends, Richard Wilding & Marie Gajewska, the collective members of The Cambridge Queen Is Dead Book Club, Cambridge 105 Radio for supporting my DJ activities, Jonathan Martin at YMCA Trinity Group, Joe & Christine Lawlor - desperate optimists, Tim Etchells, Richard Lowdon, Cathy Naden, Clair Marshall, Terry O'Connor, Robin Arthur, Jerry Gillick, John Rowley - Forced Entertainment, Keith Yon - my Voice Tutor, Rick Allsopp - my Writing Tutor at Dartington College Of Arts, Harry Robertson, my lovely mum Joan Irene Weaver, and not least of course, Max K Weaver, my very talented and beautiful son.

BV - #0027 - 161123 - C0 - 210/148/10 - PB - 9781913675288 - Matt Lamination